3.14

AN UNMARKED GRAVE

GRAVE

A Tony Boudreaux Mystery

AN UNMARKED GRAVE

•

Kent Conwell

AVALON BOOKS
NEW YORK

Published by Thomas Bouregy & Co., Inc.
160 Madison Avenue, New York, NY 10016

Library of Congress Cataloging-in-Publication Data

Conwell, Kent.
    An unmarked grave / Kent Conwell.
        p. cm.
    ISBN 978-0-8034-9969-0
    1. Boudreaux, Tony (Fictitious character)—Fiction.   2. Private
investigators—Texas—Austin—Fiction.   3. Austin (Tex.)—
Fiction.   4. Murder—Investigation—Fiction.   5. Unidentified
flying objects—Sightings and encounters—Texas—Fiction.
I. Title.

PS3553.O547U56 2009
813'.54—dc22

                                                    2009003694

PRINTED IN THE UNITED STATES OF AMERICA
ON ACID-FREE PAPER
BY HADDON CRAFTSMEN, BLOOMSBURG, PENNSYLVANIA

To Amy, who loves a good mystery.
And to my wife, Gayle.

Chapter One

"**M**istrust everyone," Marty Blevins always said.

And that was one of the first, and by far the most difficult, tenets of the PI business for me to observe. Back on my *grandpère*'s Louisiana farm, I had grown up a good little Catholic, trusting everyone, and such ingrained behavior is hard to change.

But it wasn't at all difficult to be skeptical when I heard about the UFO that had crashed into a windmill just north of Fort Worth, Texas, over a hundred years earlier. I never believed in UFOs, so when I looked into the coffin in which the alien craft's pilot had allegedly been buried, I was stunned when I spotted white skeletal remains.

The only problem was, they were not the bones of a three-foot-tall alien but of a six-foot human who had been cut in half and jammed into the small wooden casket.

At my shoulder, Jack Edney muttered a soft curse. "That sure don't look like any midget I've ever seen."

1

One thing about Jack, he had a knack for cutting to the heart of the matter.

A month earlier in Austin, my boss, Marty Blevins, had called me into his office and introduced me to Patricia Ann Chester.

I smiled and nodded, quickly taking in her appearance, which at a glance screamed money. Wearing a tan business suit, she was a tad overweight, but not a strand of her dark hair was mussed, her nails were perfectly done in a soft pink to match her lipstick, and the diamonds on her slender fingers almost blinded me. "Mrs. Chester."

She smiled becomingly. In a soft, almost inaudible voice she said, "I never married, Mr. Boudreaux." Before I could reply, she continued. "Mr. Blevins has told me about you. I hope you can help."

Arching an eyebrow at Marty, I replied. "I'll do my best, Ms. Chester."

Her eyes smiled. "Please, call me Tricia."

I liked her right away. "All right, Tricia. I'm Tony."

Marty cleared his throat. "Miss Chester wants us to locate her younger brother, Justin."

I glanced at her, wondering why someone her age, which I guessed was the upside of forty, had never married.

A slight blush colored her cheeks. "He's been missing fifteen years." She forced a self-conscious smile. "Obviously," she added apologetically, "we're not what you might call a close family, Tony."

Years in the PI business have taught be to keep a straight face, which I managed even as I pondered what I considered the understatement of the year. I remained silent.

Within my family in Church Point, Louisiana, if the older folks went a week without seeing the other members of our family around the parish, they'd wring their hands and go to confession.

Tricia continued. "I don't know if you've ever heard of Colorado Motors here in Austin, but my father owned it."

I raised an eyebrow. Who hadn't heard of Colorado Motors? "Yes."

"He passed away two weeks ago."

"Sorry," I muttered. "I read about it."

She smiled sadly. "There are four of us children—me; Frank, who is the oldest; a sister, Vanessa; and Justin. He's the youngest by ten years." She paused, staring at her hands as she twisted the rings on her perfectly manicured fingers. "Justin was always the kind who wanted to go his own way. He was a late-in-life baby. Mother died in childbirth."

And then good old Marty muttered, "I'm sorry. Which child?"

Tricia looked at me in surprise.

I know Marty meant the remark to be commiserating. More times than I could count, he had stepped neck-deep into a faux pas of unbelievable depth, and this was no exception. Smiling feebly at her, I replied to his question. "Justin, the youngest one, Marty."

"Oh." He nodded somberly, never realizing his blunder.

Taking a deep breath, I turned back to Tricia. "Fifteen years, you say? Any idea where he might be?"

She shook her head briefly. "No." She paused and added softly, "I'm sorry."

With renewed exuberance Marty replied. "Not to worry,

Ms. Chester. If he's alive, we'll find the young man for you. Isn't that right, Tony?"

I grimaced at his lack of sensitivity, but then, that was Marty.

Her eyes flickered at the momentary pain his words caused. She set her jaw. "I hope he is alive, Mr. Blevins. I hope you can find him. I am well aware that fifteen years is more than enough time for a person to hide himself if he doesn't want to be found."

I nodded. "That could be a possibility. But then again, he might want to be found."

She seemed a genuinely concerned woman. While her dress, her appearance, suggested money, I didn't know how much until she added, "Yes. My father's estate exceeds forty million dollars." Her eyes grew steely. "I want Justin to have his share."

I have no idea why I asked the question, but I did. "Is there any reason he shouldn't, providing we find him?"

Her delicately made-up cheeks blushed deeper. "My brother and sister are—" She hesitated, chewing on her bottom lip, her thin eyebrows knit. "The truth is, Tony, I don't know really how to put it other than neither would lose a night's sleep if Justin never returned. Frank suggested putting Justin's share into some kind of interest-bearing trust until he returned."

I shrugged. That didn't seem out of line until she added, "With a three-year time limit on his return."

Arching an eyebrow, I replied. "Somehow I get the feeling your older brother doesn't want to find Justin."

Her brows knit further.

Before she could reply, I asked. "What about your sister? What was her name? Vanessa?"

Tricia's face grew hard. "Vanessa wanted to have Justin declared dead twice in the last eight years. Father refused adamantly, but I have no doubt she is trying to do so now, even if it means sharing Justin's ten million with Frank and me."

Marty glanced at me with raised eyebrows. Reading his mind, I nodded. "Do they know you've come to us?"

She glanced at her hands in her lap. "No." She raised her eyes defiantly. "They have nothing to say about it. I'll cover your fee myself."

Marty shrugged. "Fine with me."

I held up a hand. "You need to tell them."

She nodded. "I know. I—I was wondering if you could be with me when I do."

Her request caught me by surprise. I stammered. "Well . . ."

Marty replied for me. "He'll be happy to, Ms. Chester."

I glared at Marty.

She beamed. "Fine. Make it around seven tonight. That's when we have evening cocktails."

Suppressing a wry smile, I dipped my head in agreement. The only time I had cocktails at seven was when I escorted Janice Coffman-Morrison, my on-again, off-again significant other, to one of her charitable soirees. Otherwise my "evening cocktail" was usually a Diet Coke or an Old Milwaukee (when I felt like ducking AA) and a hamburger at 5:45. "No problem," I replied. "See you then."

I whistled in awe when I glimpsed the Chester mansion from the highway. The sprawling residence sat on a hill overlooking Lake Travis west of Austin. At a couple minutes after seven, I pulled into the circular drive in front of a redbrick edifice that reminded me of Tara in *Gone With the Wind,* complete with a three-story portico supported by fluted Ionic columns with scrolled capitals.

A matronly woman with her gray hair pulled back into a bun opened the door. I guessed she was in her fifties. She wore a tiny lace apron over a black dress that came to just below her knees.

I introduced myself, and she nodded. "This way please," she replied succinctly, turning on her heel and leading me through a spacious foyer and hallway to an airy dayroom in the rear overlooking the lake below.

Tricia hurried to meet me, a strained smile on her face. She had changed into a simple dark blue dress with a light blue sash around the waist. She extended her hand. "Thank you for coming, Tony." She paused, then whispered, "I just told them."

I nodded with a smile, which faded when I met the cold eyes of Frank and Vanessa Chester. I forced the smile back to my lips as Tricia introduced me to her siblings.

Vanessa sat primly on the edge of a red velour wing chair, glaring at me. Her hair was almost blue-black with a white streak running down the middle. She wore a light-colored blouse and tan slacks. I couldn't help thinking of Elsa Lanchester in *The Bride of Frankenstein.* I suppressed a smile.

On the coffee table in front of her was a platter of hors d'oeuvres—some sort of vegetables with melted cheese on top.

His thick fingers cradling a cocktail, Frank Chester stood with his back to the windows overlooking the lake. Filling out a gray three-piece suit abundantly, he appeared to be in his late fifties. His gray hair gave him a look of distinction, but his florid jowls told me he had tossed down a few cocktails too many that evening.

He nodded sharply, his eyes narrowing. He inclined his head toward the coffee table. "Would you care for a snack, Mr. Boudreaux? Artichoke bruschetta. Quite delicious."

I shook my head. "No, thanks. I grabbed a bite earlier." It was a lie, but the thought of artichoke bruschetta, whatever it was, held no appeal for me. I'd eat pimento cheese before I'd take a bit of that bruschetta stuff.

He shot a wicked glance at his younger sister, then fixed his black eyes on mine. "As you wish. You should know, Mr. Boudreaux, that I heartily disapprove that Tricia engaged your company to search for my brother."

Irked by his brusque tone, I replied lightly. "After fifteen years, chances are a man doesn't want to be found. If so, it can be nearly impossible to locate him, Mr. Chester." I inclined my head toward Tricia. "I explained that to your sister earlier. And I'll tell you, chances are slim."

Frowning, he studied me for a moment. I had the distinct feeling the possibility had never occurred to him that perhaps his little brother did not want to be found.

When Tricia introduced me to Vanessa, the older woman snorted. "It's a waste of time and money. For all we know, Justin is dead. He must be, since we haven't heard from him in all these years."

In a pacifying tone, Tricia responded. "Then that's what we'll find out, Vanessa. You know that's what father would want."

The older woman's eyes flashed fire. "I know no such

thing. All I'm saying is that it's throwing good money after bad. Justin was always irresponsible, always drunk. Heaven only knows how much Father spent on bailing him out of trouble." Her face a mask of anger, she turned to me, her tone acerbic with accusation. "Did my sister tell you our father spent thousands of dollars buying Justin out of first one escapade and then another? If it wasn't drink of drugs, it was buying off angry fathers or paying DUI tickets."

Frank stepped forward. "That's enough, Vanessa. We keep our dirty laundry in the family, not out where some—" He hesitated, then continued. "Where others can see."

"But, Frank, you said yourself—"

Smoothly the older man cut her off. A sly look filled his eyes. "We say a lot of things when we're together as family, but you know, now that I think about it, perhaps Tricia has the right idea after all."

His words clearly surprised Vanessa. She started to protest, but he continued. "This way, we'll find out one way or another about Justin. If something has happened to him, then we'll legally be able to settle George's estate without any problems."

My ears perked up, and a dozen questions filled my head when he called his father by his given name.

Vanessa hesitated. "But what if he's alive?" She shot me a furtive glance.

"Then he's alive, and we can still get on with the business of settling the estate. If he doesn't want to go into the business with us, we'll buy him out. Then he can go back to whatever it is he's been doing for the last fifteen years."

The two siblings stared at each other for several moments. I've heard it said that some siblings can communicate just through eye contact. I don't know if that's true or not, for I had none. If it is, then I saw an understanding take place between Vanessa and Frank, who then turned to me. "How soon can you get started, Mr. Boudreaux?"

I had an uncomfortable feeling that this case might turn out a great deal differently than any of us expected. "Right away." I looked from one to the other and pulled out my notepad. "First I need a photo and some information about your brother."

Chapter Two

For the next thirty minutes, I picked their brains. I learned Justin's likes, dislikes, old friends, interests, and skills. Perhaps it would be better to say, lack of skills.

I studied his photo. At twenty-five, Justin Jeremy Chester, his black hair parted in the middle and hanging down to his shoulders, was as thin as the proverbial rail. There was a haunted look in his eyes, as if the poor guy was trying to find someplace he truly belonged. He had two years of college at my alma mater, the University of Texas, where his grades suggested he majored in fraternities and sororities before flunking out. I chuckled to myself. The proverbial rolling stone and good-time Charlie.

Curiously enough, one fact didn't fit with the others. After he left home, he never touched the bank account his father had set up for him.

I frowned when Tricia mentioned that fact. She explained. "Father set up bank accounts for all of us when we were in

10

school, until we were on our own. You know, so we wouldn't always be asking him for money." She paused and glanced at her brother and sister. With a glint of defiance in her eyes, she added, "He kept twenty-five thousand dollars in them. When an account got down to ten, he built it back up."

When I glanced at Frank and Vanessa, they looked away as if not wanting to admit they had enjoyed such bounty from their father.

"One other thing," I added. "It will make my search easier if I can say there is a reward for those who provide us useful information."

Vanessa looked back around sharply, her eyes blazing. "Not from my share. I—" She caught herself and looked up at her brother and sister in defiance. "Let Justin spend his own money."

So, by tacit agreement, Justin would pay for information leading to his own discovery with his own money. What a loving, supportive family!

The process of locating missing persons isn't difficult. That's why most agencies start their neophyte PIs on it.

To locate a missing person, you start with the most obvious source, the local phone book, and expand from there. That was my job with Blevins Security when I began a few years back. At that time, *tedium* was the name of the process, for many agencies had yet to tinker with computers.

I had a working knowledge of them from my days teaching English at Madison High in Austin. After several months of building my own database of sources on the computer, I became a whiz at running down skips and locating missing persons.

So, that night, when I returned to my apartment on Payton-Gin Road, I flipped on my desktop computer. While it ran through the start-up cycle, I nuked a bowl of milk for A.B., my cat, and poured him a bowl of cat nuggets. I couldn't help noticing he moved gingerly around the apartment. Who could blame him? With sympathetic reluctance, I'd had him neutered the day before.

"Sorry, old guy, but it was for the best. You're an inside cat now."

I started to pop a beer, but my conscience prevailed. I'd missed my last two AA meetings, so I was feeling guilty. Instead, I opened a can of Diet Coke.

All of my location sources were in the same folder, so it was simple to pull up a Web site, input *Justin Jeremy Chester,* and click.

Within thirty minutes I had half a dozen leads, all by that name, all forty years old, and, unfortunately, all scattered to every corner of the country. To be honest, I didn't figure any of them would bear fruit, and I was right. Within another few minutes, I crossed off the last one.

Then I started on Justin's friends, what few the three siblings could remember.

The first few I contacted were of no help whatsoever. A couple had to stop and think when I mentioned Justin's name. "Wow!" George Elkins exclaimed. "You know, I'd forgotten all about old Justin. Jeez, can you imagine?"

Then I called B. B. Cook. The name didn't register with me until I realized B. B. Cook was Bartholomew Cook, my insurance agent.

When I identified myself on the telephone, he grew

concerned. "Nothing wrong, is there, Tony? Service all right, huh?"

I laughed and explained why I had called. I guess the good Lord takes care of inept dummies like me, because Bartholomew gave me my first lead. It was over a year old, but he had heard down on Sixth Street that Justin once bussed tables on the Riverwalk in San Antonio.

A few of my database sources retrieve criminal records for a nominal fee, so within a few more minutes I discovered that—while nothing serious popped up for the last fifteen years, from the time Justin dropped out of college until he disappeared—he'd been arrested a few times, although there were no convictions. I grinned, the cynic in me seeing the handiwork of a rich father.

At that moment, the phone rang. I recognized the soft, dulcet tones of Janice Coffman-Morrison, my significant other.

"Hi, Tony."

"Janice."

We had met a few years earlier when I worked for an insurance company. I helped her out of a little jam, and we began seeing each other. Her Aunt Beatrice Morrison owned and was CEO of the Chalk Hills Distillery west of Austin.

Over the years, I escorted Janice to many of the soirees her aunt hosted. For me, a country boy from Church Point, Louisiana, to whom sitting on a riverbank fishing for *gaspergou* and *shoepick* was as close to heaven as I figured I would ever get, those affairs made me realize that even among the very rich, there are still levels of social position.

Beatrice Morrison, arguably the richest woman in Texas,

commandeered the top level. And those below strove for her approval.

Janice bubbled, "Aunt Beatrice's annual Winter Ball is in a couple weeks. You haven't forgotten, have you?"

I chuckled. "Of course not." I knew her well enough to know another shoe was about to drop.

After a pause, she added, "She wondered if you would mind preparing a bowl of Cajun gumbo for the affair, about five gallons."

There it was. I laughed. "You know I will." While Beatrice Morrison held little love for me, she worshipped the Cajun dishes I walked on—I mean, whipped up—dishes handed down by Acadians from the time of their dispersal from Nova Scotia a couple hundred years back.

"Good."

I changed the subject. "I thought you were leaving town today."

"I am. Aunt Beatrice and I are taking her private jet to Dallas for the spring fashion show at Neiman Marcus. Our wardrobes are so worn and out of style."

To my poor little rich girl, *worn* meant she had donned an article of clothing twice, three times at the most. And *out of style* meant she had purchased the item at least three months earlier.

"Well, have fun. Call when you get back."

In Austin, I know which way is north and which way is south. I've never figured out how or why, but somewhere between Austin and San Antonio, Nature gets cute and switches directions on me. I always come into San Antonio from the east, not the north. It's been that way for over twenty years.

Though I'm embarrassed to admit it, when I was a freshman at UT, several of us frat boys decided to head to Laredo for a weekend. The route cut through San Antonio. I was driving. It was late. The others were sleeping. When I hit the loop, my sense of direction turned me east toward Houston.

Fortunately I caught my error a few miles out and looped back. We made Laredo by morning, but it is most disconcerting to be driving south but feeling you're heading west.

Over the ensuing years, I'd driven to San Antonio enough to ignore my sense of direction. So midmorning the next day, without getting lost, I pulled my Silverado pickup into the parking garage of the Toreador Towers on the Riverwalk.

As always at the Toreador, as soon as I pushed through the double doors, the ringing strains of the "Toréador's Song" from Georges Bizet's opera *Carmen* blared out, ostensibly calling attention to the newest guest of the hotel.

From various sources I've heard that the "Hispanic" word *toreador* was created by the French lyricist, Bizet, for rhyming purposes. The rationale was that the word *torero* was not long enough for a verse in one of the songs in his opera. True or not, it's a neat piece of trivia to throw out when you're standing around a bar betting for drinks.

After I checked in, I headed for the Riverwalk, but not before placing a thin strand of carpet fiber between the door to my room and the jamb. I know, I know. CIA-type stuff, but the truth is, often in my line of work, I find some individuals very opposed to my carrying out my job.

For November, the weather was pleasant, and tourists strolled the quaint sidewalks.

The San Antonio Riverwalk follows the bed of the old San Antonio River more or less, wending its serpentine course through the middle of the city. High overhead, automobiles and buses crowd the streets of the city. Steep flights of stairs lead from the streets overhead to the sidewalks below.

Flagstone walks twenty feet wide line either side of the river, which itself is about thirty or so feet in width. Stone walls, decorated with striking murals portraying the history of the city, shore up the banks, and graceful pedestrian bridges of native stone arch over the river.

Through the heart of the exotic city, plush hotels, the room rates of which make me cringe, line the walk, their expansive verandas overlooking the river. Between the five-star hotels are jammed every imaginable type of restaurant, grill, coffeehouse, pizzeria, cookshack, lunch wagon, and bar.

Often, to carry out a job, PIs create a cover story, a pretext, but for this job, the truth was best. I was looking for the missing heir of a multimillion-dollar estate. If anyone provided information helping me locate the individual, they would be rewarded accordingly.

Rewards always seem to promote interest in a situation. I don't know if that's an indictment of our current society or not. All I know is that it works, and I use it every time the situation is appropriate.

Even for November, the day was warm. By noon I had visited over thirty bars and restaurants. With a long sigh, I parked my weary frame in a chair in the shadow of a large umbrella in front of the Villa hotel and, enjoying the breeze sweeping along the river, indulged in an ice-cold margarita, with, I might add, very few thoughts of and absolutely no regrets about AA.

One of the pleasures of sitting in the shade of the large umbrellas and sipping a cold drink is the chance to study the people walking by. From giggling girls in short-shorts to men in business suits, the Riverwalk hosted a smorgasbord of humanity.

Half an hour and another margarita later, I continued my search.

I hadn't taken ten steps when I jerked to a halt and peered across the river at a woman on the patio of Beamer's Bourbons. She wore a pale blue sleeveless sheath dress with a darker belt about her slender waist.

My ex-wife, Diane.

Chapter Three

I called out to her. When she looked around, I waved. At first she frowned; then, when she recognized me, she motioned me over.

Diane and I had parted amicably years before. We'd been high school sweethearts and married right after graduation, but within a short time the everyday grind of a much-too-soon marriage slowly erased the rosy blush of young love. Fortunately, we had no children, only an aquarium of exotic fish.

I got the fish, she got everything else, and we were both happy. She left Austin, and I lost touch with her. A few years later I found her in Vicksburg, where I had accompanied my old friend Jack Edney to the reading of his father's will. Jack, who was a high school coach when I was teaching English, ended up with several million dollars.

The next year, Diane showed up in Austin, and, not

wanting to become involved with her again, I introduced her to Jack. They hit it off and just recently married.

I had my doubts about the marriage. I read somewhere that the most important thing in a marriage was that one of the partners should be willing to take orders. And neither Diane nor Jack fit into that category. So the ensuing fireworks never surprised me.

Diane smiled up at me and, stretching her swanlike neck, lifted her cheek for me to kiss.

"Hey," I said, looking around. "Where's that husband of yours?"

Her face turned sour. "I don't know, and I don't care!"

Now, I might be slow, but I didn't come out of the turnip patch last night. Reluctantly I asked, "Trouble?"

Her eyes blazed. "I don't want to talk about it!"

Inwardly I grimaced. I had stumbled into the middle of a marital quagmire that could get dicey. I nodded. "Okay. What do we talk about?" I glanced across the river and spotted a man in a tan business suit seated at a table and reading a newspaper. He looked like a bulldog, and he was staring at us. When he spotted me, he quickly turned back to his paper. I thought nothing of it—something I would later remember.

She shrugged and drained her bourbon. She plopped the glass down onto the table. "Another one. A double." Her brown eyes stared at me in defiance.

"No problem." I held up an arm and pointed to her glass with two fingers. The young waitress dipped her head and moments later slid another double bourbon in front of Diane.

By now I was wishing I had never spotted her. She was fast approaching the tipsy level, and from the sullen expression on her face, she would not stop until she hit the wiped-out stage.

She gulped a large belt and looked up at me. "What are you doing here? Work?"

With an indifferent shrug I replied, "Yep. You know how it is. Trying to find a guy."

"Where are you staying?"

"At the Toreador." I should have expected what was to come next, but I didn't.

Pursing her lips, she leaned forward, studying me. Her eyes grew sultry, which, to be honest, unnerved me. "Do you miss being married to me, Tony?"

The question knocked me back in my chair. I stammered for words. "Why, uh—uh—yeah." I gave her a crooked grin and tried to laugh her question off. "Just like you miss being married to a slob like me." I congratulated myself on what I thought was a snappy answer that would cut off any further uncomfortable questions.

She leaned closer, her eyes cloudy. With a sly smile on her lips, she whispered, "Why don't we go back to your room?"

Talk about stammering. I finally managed to mumble, "Good joke, Diane. You had me going." I glanced at my watch and pushed back from the table. "Besides, I have to meet a guy at twelve-thirty. It's almost that time now."

"Hey, Tony!"

I looked around and spotted Jack coming out of the bar in our direction. I went limp with relief. He grabbed my hand and shook it. "How you been?"

Diane glared up at him. If I've ever seen daggers coming out of someone's eyes, it was hers.

Jack, who always reminded me of a jovial bowling ball, gestured to my chair. "Sit. Have lunch with us."

I begged off. "Like I told Diane, I've got to meet a guy." I started backing away. "Good to see the two of you again. Take care."

I didn't look back for half a block. When I did, I spotted Diane storming off with Jack on her heels, his arms spread in supplication.

Turning back around, I spotted the man in the tan business suit peering into the window of a curio shop. Even from the side he looked like a bulldog with those flopping jowls.

My luck on the Riverwalk was going from bad to worse until I hit Elena's, a small bar. There was only one customer when I entered. At one end of the bar was a small stage for the nightly music group.

The bartender was named Narelle, an attractive woman who looked to be in her late twenties, but I decided she was in her forties when she commented that Elena's nightly bands were good but nothing like Thin Lizzy.

I slid onto a stool and showed her the snapshot of Justin Chester. I laughed. "It's about fifteen years old, so sort of use your imagination."

Chewing on her bottom lip, she studied the photo. "Nope, but I tell you, Jig comes on at eight. He runs the bar until we close."

"Jig?"

"Yeah. Eddie Grimes. He's been around forever. Maybe he'll recognize your friend."

I tapped the snapshot in the palm of my hand. "This guy

here stands to inherit a large amount of money. There's a reward."

Narelle arched an eyebrow. "How much is the inheritance?"

With a grin, I replied, "Ten million."

Her jaw dropped open. Then she gave me a sly grin. "Would you believe me if I told you I was his wife?"

I laughed. "Come on, Narelle. You can do better than that."

She chuckled and wiped the bar. "Can't blame a gal for trying." She paused and shook her head. "Ten million. Some guys have all the luck."

Later, I would see the irony in her remark.

Outside, I glanced at my watch. Six-thirty. My stomach growled. Street lamps along the Riverwalk punched warm holes in the growing dusk. To the west, the last remnants of purple and orange clouds painted the brittle blue sky in broad swaths.

Crossing the river, I headed back to the hotel. On impulse, I stopped at a sidewalk restaurant for an icy mug of beer and a platter of chicken quesadillas.

I sipped the beer and leaned back. I stretched my arms over my head. The day had not proven too profitable, but I knew from experience, what looked hopeless at one moment could be encouraging the next. I had allocated three days to the Riverwalk. In addition to the business establishments, there were hundreds of vendors plying their trade along the boulevard of tourists, selling everything from shoeshines to homemade pralines.

A few minutes before eight, I noticed a crowd of tourists

gathering at the foot of the steep flight of stairs leading up to Houston Street high overhead.

Idly I watched, curious. The crowd grew.

Minutes later the crowd parted as an ambulance pulled up. Shortly, it departed, winding along the walk to the emergency ramp leading to the streets above.

A few minutes after eight, I pushed through the doors into Elena's, which by now was crowded. A four-piece group sat on the stamp-sized stage, readying for their first set. I elbowed my way to the bar and spotted Narelle. I nodded. "Jig around?"

The smile on her face faded. "He had an accident."

I frowned at her. "Accident?"

She arched an eyebrow. In disgust she replied, "Must have had too much to drink. He fell down the Houston Street stairs." She inclined her head in the direction of the other bartender. "Rudy said he heard Jig busted a leg." She shook her head and muttered a curse as she drew three beers. "The idiot put a crimp in a whole lot of my plans. I had a long weekend all laid out too. Now I'll have to be in this dump."

I couldn't believe my ears. "What hospital? Any idea?"

She shrugged. "Probably Christus St. Mary's. That's where they usually take them."

"How do I get there?"

She paused in drawing the beer and looked curiously at me. "You going over there?"

"Why not? Worst that can happen is they won't let me see him."

Pointing south, she said, "Six blocks to the corner of Navarro and St. Mary's. Can't miss it."

I winked. "Thanks."

"And, hey," she yelled, "don't forget I told you about Jig if you find that guy."

"Don't worry."

Half a dozen gurneys with groaning patients filled the ER. Medical personnel bustled back and forth. I stopped a young man in a white jacket, jeans, and running shoes. "Do you have a guy named Jig?"

"Jig?" The young intern frowned.

"Eddie Grimes. He fell down the stairs at the Houston Street Bridge over the Riverwalk."

His face lit up. "Oh, that one. The old drunk." He pointed to a small, baldheaded man on a gurney next to a wall, his face taut with pain. "That's him there."

"May I talk to him a moment? See if he needs anything from home?"

The young doctor studied me a moment. "Family? Sure. Go ahead."

I hurried across the room. "Jig? Jig? You hear me?"

A wizened little man, he appeared to be in his sixties or so. He cracked his eyes open and peered up at me. "Who— Who are you?"

The booze on his breath knocked me back a step. "Narelle, back at the bar, sent me. Said you could help me and maybe pick up some money doing it."

He closed his eyes and slowly shook his head. "Go away. I hurt too bad."

I leaned down and whispered, "Might be up to ten thousand dollars in it for you."

His eyes popped open. He looked at me in disbelief.

Quickly I explained why I was there, then showed him the snapshot of Justin Chester.

His eyes grew wide, and he frowned. "I told the other guy. Didn't he tell you?"

His words stunned me. "What other guy? Tell him what?"

"He didn't say nothing about a reward."

My brain raced. "Someone else showed you this picture?"

"Naw. Not that one, another one. What about the reward?"

"Ten thousand, Jig. If I can find this guy in the picture. You know him?"

"Justin? Sure, I do. I—"

At that moment a matronly nurse stopped at the gurney. "How's the pain, Mr. Grimes?"

He bit his lip and shook his head. "Still hurts bad."

She quickly drew a syringe and gave him another shot of painkiller.

After she left, I asked Jig, "Do you know where I can find Justin?"

"Like I told the other guy, one of the band members that played at our bar a few months ago did a gig at some country club in Fort Worth. He spotted Justin up there. They shot the breeze a few minutes."

"Who is this guy?"

Jig stared at me blankly, then blinked once or twice. "I just knew him as Bones."

"What about the name of the band?"

"Let me see . . . It was some drink—Grasshoppers, I think."

"You remember the name of the country club?"

His eyes started drooping from the drugs the nurse had administered. "Naw." His words slurring now, he muttered, "Don't forget my reward."

"I won't. And you be careful on those stairs. Your bones are too brittle to fall down them again."

Dragging the tip of his tongue across his dry lips, he mumbled, "Didn't fall. Somebody pushed me. Didn't see who."

Chapter Four

I stared at him in disbelief. Had someone pushed him, or had he just stumbled? If someone did, who? Could it have been the man who had asked him about Justin? And even if it were, why try to kill the old man?

I had a head filled with a bucketful of questions and no answers.

I tried to rouse Jig, but the drugs had taken effect. Not even the offer of free whiskey could wake him.

Outside the hospital, I hailed a cab and headed back to the hotel.

As I entered the lobby to the rousing strains of the "Toréador's Song," I spotted the man in the tan business suit exiting the lobby on the Riverwalk side.

I took the stairs instead of the elevator. It was almost nine. By the time I cleaned up and put together all my notes, it would be time for bed. I wanted to rise early and get back to Austin before heading on up to Fort Worth.

Pausing before I opened the door to my room, I spotted the carpet fiber on the floor. Someone had been in my room. For all I knew, he or she might still be there.

Opening the door slowly, I slipped my hand inside and flipped on the light. After a few moments of silence, I pushed the door wide open and surveyed the room.

Empty!

Nothing seemed to be disturbed.

Drawing a deep breath and releasing it slowly, I closed and locked the door.

After showering, I pulled out my notes and transferred them to index cards—one incident, one card. I learned long ago from Al Grogan, the resident Sherlock Holmes of Blevins Security, that by writing one idea per card, it was simple to rearrange ideas to gain a different perspective on the case. Sometimes it proved effective, sometimes it didn't.

Around midnight, I called the desk and left a 5:00 A.M. wake-up call. After climbing between the sheets on a bed that must have been carved out of the limestone hills surrounding San Antonio, I lay staring at the ceiling, listening to a muted cacophony of voices and traffic.

All things considered, the day had proven to be worthwhile. I'd picked up another lead on Justin Chester; however, the fact that someone else was also searching for him puzzled me. And to add to the puzzle, had that someone attempted to kill Jig Grimes? Or was that just the old man's drunken imagination? I opted for the latter.

I shook my head. One fact was certain: there were two of us looking for Justin Chester. Who had hired the second one?

* * *

The buzzing of the telephone awakened me. I couldn't believe it was already 5:00 A.M. It seemed as if I had just dropped off.

"Hello."

Jack Edney's strident voice cut through my drowsiness. "Tony, it's Jack. Did I wake you?"

I blinked my eyes at the clock. Twelve-thirty. I groaned. "What's wrong?"

"Diane left me. She took the Cadillac and left me stranded."

My eyes drifted shut. "So? You're a millionaire. Hire a taxi to take you back to Austin."

"Sure. Hey, are you going to be around tomorrow?"

When you're groggy with sleep, your brain doesn't function fast enough to tell a lie. "No. I finished my job here."

"Great. How about a ride home tomorrow? What time you leaving?"

"As soon after five as I can."

"Great. I'll be in the lobby, okay? See you then."

"Yeah, okay," I muttered, hanging up the receiver and instantly dropping into deep slumber.

True to his word, Jack Edney was waiting in the lobby the next morning, bright-eyed. We pulled onto I-35 a few minutes later, heading for Austin, pulling off once at a Mc-Donald's for a carryout breakfast.

With the drive to Austin taking almost ninety minutes, I figured on sorting my thoughts and planning my next few steps. Instead, I listened to an hour and half of Jack's troubles. "How long were you two married?" he asked as we pulled on to Ben White Road in Austin.

I shrugged. "A couple years."

"What happened?"

"Beats me. We just became different. Married too young, I suppose."

He clucked his tongue and looked down the highway. "Did she spend money like she does now?"

I couldn't help laughing. "We didn't have any." I glanced at him.

He read the question in my eyes. "She spends like there's no tomorrow, and when I question her about it, she pouts." He rolled his eyes. "I've never seen a woman pout like she can."

After dropping Jack off at his office on Highway 290 West, I headed up Lamar to my own office, a cubbyhole at Blevins Security. I figured a few phone calls would save me a lot of running around when I hit Fort Worth.

I don't know if it is an undiscovered law of nature or not, but when most people find out they're talking to a private investigator on the telephone, their memory short-circuits. Early in my career, I butted heads with that phenomenon a dozen times before I learned how to avoid it. I simply lied.

My lie this time was that I was a prospective employer calling to verify Justin Chester's last employment. Personnel officers seem to feel a kinship with others in their field, so they're usually somewhat more accommodating.

Introducing myself as J. B. Forester, I began calling the country clubs in Fort Worth. My first two calls were fruitless. On the third one, luck latched on to my shirttail. Wilson Adams, personnel manager at the Brentwood Country Club, informed me that Justin Chester had worked at their club for six months. He gave notice the previous June.

"Did he give any indication where he was heading, Mr. Adams?"

Adams hesitated. "No." Then, suspicious, he asked, "Isn't it on his application?"

Glibly I replied. "No. There's a six-month gap in his employment history."

My response satisfied him. "He didn't mention anything. He just came in one day and gave his notice. I hated to lose him." He paused and added, "I never could figure him out."

"Oh? How's that?"

"Well, his age for one thing. He was around forty. That's old for a busboy, but he was always conscientious and always did a good job. In fact," he added, "the younger busboys worked harder just so an old man wouldn't show them up." He laughed. "Crazy, huh?"

Despite being disappointed in the dead end, I laughed with him. "Yeah."

He changed the subject. "Who did you say you were?"

"J. B. Forester. Hammond Electronics."

There was a moment of silence; then he asked, "Was that other man one of your people?"

I stiffened and then, in as calm a voice as I could muster, replied. "This is the only contact Hammond Electronics has made with you, Mr. Adams. Why?"

He shrugged it off. "No particular reason. One of my wait staff said some guy came through asking about Justin."

I remembered the man in the tan business suit. If I asked questions about the man, I might stir up Adams' curiosity, which I didn't want to do. "Chester probably applied to another company also. Our company is a low-key vendor for the US government, Mr. Adams. For security measures, I need to find out about the six-month gap."

"Just ask Justin."

"Oh, I plan on it, but I'd like to verify whatever he says by an independent source."

"I understand."

Trying to sound as beseeching as possible, I said, "I wonder if it would be too much of an inconvenience for you if I visited with some of your kitchen or wait staff. Perhaps Justin mentioned his plans to them."

I held my breath.

"No. Be fine with me."

"Great. What about tomorrow? Around one?"

"See you then."

Marty popped into my cubicle as I hung up. I brought him up to date.

He nodded. "You know where they are? I mean, that music group, the Grasshoppers?"

"I didn't ask. I figured if I didn't learn anything from the country club, then I could pursue Bones and the Grasshoppers." I drew a deep breath and shut down my computer. "I'll run up to Fort Worth in the morning and visit with the people he worked with. No one can work side by side with someone for six months and not reveal something."

Marty arched an eyebrow. "You want to bet?"

Chapter Five

It's a good thing I didn't bet with Marty. I would have lost. The kitchen and wait staff at Brentwood was cordial and outgoing. They liked Justin, but he was a loner, never revealing any personal information about himself.

I was standing in the doorway opening into the ballroom with Jerry Byrne, one of the wait staff. An older man, he carried himself with the demeanor of a professional. He shook his head. "Sorry I couldn't tell you anything, Mr. Forester. But, like I said, Justin was all business. The only reason I knew he was from Texas was his drawl." He chuckled.

"One more question. Mr. Adams mentioned that another gentleman had inquired about Justin."

He nodded. "Yeah. Justin's sure popular."

I grinned sheepishly. "Well, I might have bothered you for nothing, Jerry. The guy might have been one of our boys, Larry Charles." I touched my fingers to my face. "Ugly."

Jerry laughed. "I didn't want to say it, but, yeah. Boy,

and I thought I had a kisser that would turn a woman to stone."

I laughed with him. "Larry's good-natured about it. Has to be." I drew a deep breath. All that was left now was Bones and the Grasshoppers. I nodded to the club employees arranging tables around the stage. "Looks like a big blowout, huh?"

Jerry rolled his eyes. "Teen night. One of those awful music groups that thinks loud is the same as good."

With a grimace, I replied, "I know what you mean." I paused, then added. "My brother's son plays for one of those groups, the Grasshoppers. You ever heard of them?"

It was his turn to roll his eyes. "Oh, do I remember them. Last spring. Prom night. My ears rang for two weeks."

Casually I asked, "Wonder if they're around anywhere. I wouldn't mind stopping in and saying hi to my nephew."

Arching his eyebrows, he replied, "I wouldn't know, but come with me. There's always teenagers in the heated pool. They'll know."

I frowned. "Teenagers? Aren't they in school?"

A wry grin twisted his lips. "These are rich kids, Mr. Forester. They go to private schools. You know what I mean?"

Unfortunately, I did.

Bones and the Grasshoppers were playing a week's gig at the Vegas Club in Dallas, named after the infamous Jack Ruby's club back in the sixties.

From where I parked, two blocks away, I could hear the band pounding away. I was surprised the walls didn't vibrate into a pile of brick dust. The club was jammed, and on the dance floor, heads, arms, and legs bobbed up and down and around.

Other than the club owners, I didn't see anyone who looked over twenty-one, yet cigarette smoke filled the room like a thick fog, and I didn't see one table that didn't have beer, wine, whiskey, or pills on it. I couldn't resist the cynical observation that perhaps somewhere in this milieu of smoke and booze was the president of the United States in thirty years.

They say beauty is in the eye of the beholder. I suppose the same could be said about music—that its beauty is in the ear of the listener.

If loud implied good, the group was great.

Somehow from my spot next to the rear wall, I managed to tolerate the reverberations until the band's first break.

A bouncer stopped me when I tried to go backstage. "No outsiders," he growled. Two twenties made me an insider.

In the dressing room, the five musicians were slouched on couches and sprawled on cots, eyes glazed, features slack, gathering their inspiration by toking on joints.

They paid me no attention. I spoke up. "First, I'm not a cop. I'm a friend of Justin Chester, and I'm looking for a gentleman called Bones."

No response.

Finally a thin, black man with long fingers rolled his head to one side. He was one of those whose age was impossible to guess. He could have been anywhere between twenty-five and seventy-five. "Well, I ain't no gentleman, boss, but I'm Bones."

I quickly explained the inheritance. When I mentioned Justin's share was ten million and there would in all likelihood be a reward, Bones grew interested. "What do I gots to do for the money?"

I shrugged. "I've got to find him. When your group played at the Brentwood Country Club last spring, you talked to him. Remember?"

Bones' blue-black forehead wrinkled in a frown. "Yeah. I remembers. Done forgot about it, but now I remembers."

"Did he give you any idea what his plans were, where he might go?"

Two of the other musicians snickered. One muttered sarcastically, "That the crazy honky, Bones?"

Bones grinned and tapped the side of his head. "Aw, the guy's okay. Just a little far out."

The other musician snorted. "Loony-tunes, if you ask me."

I frowned. "Far out?"

"Yeah. He's into all this far-out stuff like UFOs and aliens and all that weird stuff. Always been that way."

"You known him long?"

"Yeah, man. I knows him back in Austin before he ups and leaves. Over the years, I see him about. Last time was at the country club."

"Any idea where he might be?"

He squinted at me through eyes covered with a gray film. "Reckon I do. What's in it for me?"

"I'm a PI." I handed him my card. "I don't know how much, but there will be rewards to those who help me find him."

Nodding slowly, Bones cleared his throat. "When I last talked to the boy, he tells me about a place called Elysian

Hills, somewhere north of Fort Worth." He grunted and shook his head. "He must've had too much booze, 'cause he claimed a spaceship landed there over a hundred years ago and the town buried the pilot in the town cemetery." He toked again. His glazed eyes lost their focus. "I didn't believe him. He's done talked all about those things for years. You might find him up there."

"Thanks."

"Just don't forget who told you."

"No sweat. How do I get in touch with you?"

"O'Brien Agency here in Dallas. They can find us."

I started to leave, then turned back. "Has anyone else asked you about Justin lately?"

He squinted at me, a frown on his forehead. "No. Why?"

"Just wondering."

At that moment, a stagehand stuck his head in. "Showtime, fellas."

Just as I hit I-35 in downtown Dallas and headed northwest, I glanced at the dash clock. It was almost one, so beyond the city limits I pulled into a Day's Inn motel. After compiling my notes for the day, I climbed between the sheets.

Next morning, after checking out, I pulled into a Valero self-service station next door to fuel up. Behind the station ran some railroad tracks. While the tank filled, I idly watched a slow-moving train of coal cars with open top hoppers, acid cars, and boxcars clattering past, heading northwest.

As I entered the on-ramp to the interstate, I glanced at the train one last time—and froze. I blinked my eyes and squinted at the hobos hopping into the open door of an empty boxcar and disappearing back into the shadows.

The face had disappeared. Or maybe I had just imagined it. Still, I drove along the shoulder of the interstate, matching the freight's speed and sneaking glances at the open door.

At first, I thought I had spotted my old man, John Roney Boudreaux, who left Mom and me when I was around seven. Over the years, I'd run across him a few times. Last time I spotted him was in the French Quarter in New Orleans a few months earlier.

I never ceased to be amazed how the old man managed to stay alive all those years bumming across the country. While he is my father, and I have helped him several times over the years, if anyone existed who personified amorality, it was he.

He believed in and only in John Roney. All others existed to benefit him. I was in my midthirties before I finally accepted his nature and stopped lying to myself and making excuses for him. That's why the few times he stayed with me, I never felt a single pang of guilt about locking various items in the garage so he couldn't pawn them.

After a few miles, I pulled back to the inside lane and kicked my Silverado up to the speed limit.

Elysian Hills lay in the rolling hills and Post Oak Savannah sixty miles or so north of Fort Worth. It was a small community stretching for half a mile or so on either side of Farm to Market Road 1287. On both sides of the macadam road, horses and cattle grazed in pastures dotted with oil wells pumping the proverbial black gold from the earth.

I looked out over the pastoral hills, remembering my Greek mythology. The Elysian Fields were the final resting place of the souls of the virtuous and heroic. Mythology located the fields on the western fringe of the earth. The relatives of the gods were transported, without tasting death, there to the immortality of heaven. Those less fortunate skirted Elysian to face the perpetual torment of purgatory in the Fields of Asphodel.

Not to my surprise, I would once again witness the fact that sometimes the Fields of Asphodel lapped over into those of Elysian more than one wanted to believe.

The old clapboard homes sitting on the crest of hills indicated the area had at one time been a successful farming community. The newer brick homes pointed to a burgeoning bedroom community, a short drive, by Texas standards, from the Fort Worth-Dallas metroplex.

I drove slowly through the community, noting two convenience stores, three churches, a small school, a feed and tack store, a welding shop, a lube shop, an automotive garage, sheriff's office, and, to my surprise, an old green building of concrete blocks with a sign in front that read:

UFO MUSEUM,
OPEN TUES. AND THURS. 12–3.

I turned around and headed back, pulling in at the sheriff's office. The tan metal building housing the office was one of those prefabricated, cream-colored buildings so ubiquitous along the side of the road today.

A mature receptionist smiled up at me. "Yes, sir?"

Glancing around, I spotted a nameplate over a door. SHERIFF PERRY.

"My name's Tony Boudreaux. I'd like to see Sheriff Perry if I might."

She nodded and picked up the phone. Moments later she nodded to the door. "In there, sir."

A redheaded man in his late sixties with bony shoulders the width of an axe handle looked up from a desk when I entered. His hands were red, his neck was red, his face was red, and even the freckles on his face were red. I suppressed a smile when the random thought darted through my mind that if anyone deserved the nickname Red, it was he.

In a guttural voice, he said. "Yes, sir?"

"Sheriff Perry?"

He nodded. "Yeah."

I introduced myself and pulled out the snapshot of Justin Chester. I quickly explained about the inheritance. "I heard he might be around here."

Perry studied the photo, his frowning face a field of wrinkles, then handed it back to me. "I haven't seen any long-haired hippies like him around. Of course, every day more and more city folk are moving in. He might be one of them."

I shrugged. "Might be. You know, one guy over in Dallas told me that Chester was interested in UFOs and that one was supposed to have landed around here. He said the pilot was buried in your cemetery."

Perry stared at me a moment; then a wry grin creased his craggy face. "Hoax. Over a hundred years ago Elysian Hills was a big town, but the post office was moved to Reuben, and we started losing population. The mayor and a couple other of the town fathers made up the story."

Back on the highway, I pulled in at the first convenience store on my side of the highway, Hooker's.

Inside, I stopped in front of the checkout counter that sat in the middle of the store. Several newspapers with the banner *The Rueben Journal* were stacked next to the cash register. On one side of the store were grocery items and, on the other, a lunch counter and several tables, around two of which were seated several old-timers sipping coffee, perusing the *Journal,* and idly chatting.

It brought back memories of my youth in Church Point before my old man ran out on us. When it came to farm work, he left it all to his pa, my *grandpère,* Moise Boudreaux. Whenever Mom or PawPaw wanted John Roney, they could find him at the pool hall, playing forty-two or dominos.

The old-timers shot me a glance, then turned back to their discussion.

A matronly woman in jeans and an oversized sweatshirt nodded from behind the lunch counter. She wore no lipstick or nail polish. Liver spots covered her hands. Her gray-flecked hair was pulled back into a ponytail bound with a red band bearing the Confederate stars. "Be right with you, mister."

Wiping her hands on a dish towel, she hurried over. With a wide grin on her plump face, she bubbled, "Howdy, stranger. Welcome to Hooker's. I'm Mabel Hooker. What can I do for you?"

Handing her the snapshot of Justin Chester, I said, "Would you happen to recognize this gentleman, Mabel?"

Her smile faded. Her brow knit as she tentatively took the picture. She studied the photo. "I don't know."

"He was fifteen years younger there. Could have changed his whole look." I paused, then added, "And I'm not the law. His father passed away, and the family wants me to find him."

She studied it again, then ambled over to the crowded tables and handed around the photo. A roar of laughter erupted from the tables, a roar that puzzled me.

With the smile back on her face, she returned. "Finas over there says that, without the long hair, this fellow favors the janitor down at the school." She handed me the picture. "I guess he does business down the road at Fuqua's. I don't know him. Finas over there can tell you more about him."

All the old-timers were watching me as I approached. I nodded. "Good morning, gents. Which one of you is Finas?" I searched their faces.

A weathered old man in khakis and a blue jean jacket grunted. "That's me." He pointed to the picture in my hand. "You must be from the loony bin."

Chapter Six

The others roared with laughter again.

I grinned sheepishly. "Why? Should I be?"

A second old farmer spoke up. "We reckoned you was, if you be looking for Chester there."

The third one joined in. "Maybe he ought to see old Harlan Barton. Take the two in together."

They all laughed again.

Thinking back to what Bones had said, I replied, "You mean about the UFO stuff?"

For a fleeting moment, the merriment in their eyes cooled but then rekindled as one responded, "Yeah."

I hooked a thumb over my shoulder in the direction of the museum. "Don't you have a museum down the road about the UFO? I figure you might get your little town some tourists that way."

"A few, but they don't stay long."

Finas snorted at his friend. "Look at what we got over there, Carl. How long would you stay?"

Carl grinned and held up his thumb and forefinger half an inch apart. "About this long."

They all laughed again.

Another old-timer spoke up. "Mr. Chester there—he a friend of yours?"

"Nope. I work for a private security firm in Austin. Mr. Chester's father passed away. The family hired me to find him."

The laughter fled their faces. Finas spoke up. "Sorry to hear that." He gestured down the highway. "Mr. Chester works down at Elysian Hills Elementary School. You can catch him down there." He looked across the room at Mabel. "What's the principal's name down there, Mabel? I forget."

She snorted. "You ain't forgot, Finas. She's your daughter-in-law. Georgiana Irvin."

Finas grinned and chuckled, drawing another round of laughter from his cronies. "Maybe that's why I forgot. Yeah, Georgiana Irvin. She's the principal."

Eyes twinkling in mischief, the old man at Finas' elbow spoke up. "Just tell Georgiana that Finas sent you. She'll make you real welcome."

They all laughed.

I laughed with them and replied, "I was born looking like this, fellows, but I ain't that dumb."

They roared again. They were my kind of folks.

Georgiana Irvin greeted me graciously, gesturing to one of the two chairs in front of her desk. When I explained my job and that a sizeable inheritance awaited Justin Chester, she nodded slowly. "Justin is an excellent employee. I certainly would hate to lose him." She paused, and her eyes looked through me into the past. "Would you believe," she said, "I found him sleeping in our boiler room?"

When she saw the surprise on my face, she continued. "I thought he was a bum, but when he explained that he was just a footloose man looking for work, I had second thoughts. He was clean, well educated, and I needed a custodian. I had the sheriff check for any criminal records. There was none. Oh, I think one or two minor infractions years ago, but nothing else."

She continued talking, but I was scrolling back in my mind to an hour earlier, when the sheriff had denied knowing Justin Chester. Why?

"Anyway," Georgiana said, "I offered him the job, and he took it. He's been a delight to work with. I hate to lose him, but I'm thrilled by his good fortune." She frowned, realizing what she had said. "I don't mean about the death of his father, but—"

I grinned. "I know exactly what you mean. Now, would it be possible for me to see him?"

Five minutes later, a light knock sounded at the door. It opened, and a secretary looked in. "Justin's here, Georgiana."

"Send him in."

If anything, Justin Chester had grown thinner. His hair was close-cropped, and a tentative smile on his thin lips replaced the haunted look in his eyes from the photo. In a way, he looked content.

After Georgiana introduced us, she left us alone.

I sat, and Justin took the second chair. He was perplexed. "A private investigator? I don't understand."

Succinctly, I explained why I was there.

His brow knit in pain when I told him of his father. Resting his elbows on the chair arms, he leaned back and stared through me. "I wasn't a very good son, Mr. Boudreaux. I tried, but I could never make my father proud of me. I never meant to worry anyone."

I've made so many mistakes in my life that the last thing I would do is judge anyone else's behavior. "I suppose when they couldn't find you, they feared the worst," I said simply.

He gave me a shrewd look that told me he was much more perceptive than he let on. "I never tried to hide from anyone. I used my own name, driver's license, Social Security number, and sometimes even had telephone and electric service. No, they didn't want to find me." He hastened to add, "I don't blame them for that. I know you're supposed to love your brothers and sisters, but mine—well, it was really hard. So we just all sort of ended up going our separate ways."

Trying to bring a note of levity into the conversation, I replied, "Well, with your inheritance, you can certainly do that. Any ideas what you will do?"

To my surprise, he answered almost immediately. "Oh, yes. I'll come back here."

"Mrs. Irvin says you're a model employee."

His face grew warm. "I like the kids. At that age, they accept a person for who he is. Makes no difference if you're rich or poor, important or not—any of those things. But I wouldn't come back to work here."

His reply puzzled me. "Oh, then why come back here?"

He looked at me as if he couldn't believe I could ask

such a question. "Why, to find the pilot of the UFO that crashed here in 1897."

I whistled to myself, thinking that the old codgers back at Hooker's might not have been too far off on their suppositions regarding Justin Chester.

Justin lived in a small underground room behind the museum. We had to climb down a short flight of eight or ten steps to reach it. I sat on his cot while he packed what little he possessed into a worn sports bag. When he saw me looking at the bag, he grinned and with great pride said, "Would you believe, someone threw that away? I found it beside the road."

What could I say? "Not bad."

As I looked on, he removed a two-by-four from the closet doorjamb and pulled out a few bills and slid them into his wallet. He grinned sheepishly. "My 'safe.' The door doesn't have a lock, and as much as I hate to admit it, we do have people passing through who aren't above taking something that doesn't belong to them." He fit the two-by-four back into place and, stepping back, surveyed the tiny room. "That's it."

His only mode of transportation was a bicycle, so we tossed it along with his bag into the back of my pickup.

By now we were on a first-name basis. I wanted to top off the gas tank before we pulled out. Justin sent me to Fuqua's Stop and Shop, the second convenience store in Elysian Hills. While the tank was filling, I called Tricia and told her we'd be in at around six or seven.

When I went inside to pay, Justin was talking excitedly with the older man behind the register. When he spotted me, he introduced us. "Tony, this is Sam Fuqua. I've known him ever since I came here a few months ago. I was telling Sam that after I get my inheritance, I'm coming back here to find the Martian pilot they buried out at the cemetery."

"Nice to meet you, Sam," I replied, handing him my credit card and ignoring Justin's conversation with the elderly man.

As we pulled out onto the road for Austin, Justin Chester sat silently, staring blankly out the passenger window. He mumbled, "These are fine folks out here. The salt of the earth. Even if I don't find the pilot, I might just stay here anyway."

I made the mistake of asking him about the UFO.

He scooted around in the seat, his eyes alight with enthusiasm. Right before my eyes, his shyness morphed into animated exuberance.

Words tumbled from his lips, and for the next six hours, all the way back to Austin, I learned more about the mysterious UFO than I wanted to know. "It all started in April, 1897. April nineteenth, to be exact. A slow-moving spaceship crashed into a windmill. You remember seeing the house on the hill behind the museum?"

When I nodded, he continued. "That hill just east of it is where the windmill stood. Anyway, the ship broke into hundreds of pieces. When the people searched through the wreckage, the story goes they found a small body with a big head. The townsfolk gave the little man a proper burial in the local cemetery. Some of the pieces of the ship had some sort of hieroglyphics or symbols on them. There was even a write-up in a Dallas paper."

I listened with both appropriate interest and equally appropriate reservations.

My reservations grew as Justin, caught up in the enthusiasm of his mission in life, spoke of the Changing World Order, then The False Green Gospel, and finally ended up bogged down in Signs of the Last Days.

I had a friend who believed in those sort of far-out theories and initiatives. To his disappointment, the world had not come to an end the eight times he had prepared for it. In his attic, he had stored crates of Ramen noodles, cases of tinned meat, and so many five-gallon containers of water that the ceiling over the bathroom gave way.

Unfortunately, he was in the tub at the time and got his arm snapped in two spots. But he still believes. Don't ever doubt that for every sane person, there aren't at least five kooks. Once, I heard someone say they'd known people as nutty as a granola bar. And that was a problem with no solution, for even if you took out the nuts and fruit, what you still had left were the flakes. At that moment, my opinion of Justin Chester was swinging in the same direction.

He must have spotted the wry curl of my lips. "You don't believe me, do you?"

With a shrug, I passed it off. "Never really thought about it, Justin. It's an interesting concept."

"It's more than interesting."

I glanced at him.

He was animated, bouncing with excitement and exuding a vibrant enthusiasm. He continued. "In 1948, back before our time, the United Nations was formed. Right?"

I grinned sheepishly and flexed my fingers on the wheel. "I'll take your word for it."

"Well, it was, and then Israel was given world recognition.

As an independent nation, the country fulfilled the prophecy that, in the years to come, she would be a world player."

Now I was growing uncomfortable. "I never heard that."

"It's true. It was a Biblical prophecy."

"Okay." I crossed my fingers that his lecture was over, but I was disappointed. He was just getting started.

"To top everything off, today, ethical and moral values are collapsing, and science is making greater gains in one year than in the entire previous century."

I could feel his eyes boring into the side of my head.

In a somber voice, he added. "Those are the Signs of the Last Days."

"So," not knowing what else to say, I asked, "how does that tie into the UFO business?"

"It's all part of it. The UFOs and the Changing World Order." He paused and studied me, seeing the skepticism in my eyes. "You don't believe me, do you?"

"Well, I—"

He interrupted. "That's all right. With the inheritance, I can buy equipment that will help me prove the UFO existed, and when I do, you'll be the first one I call. Okay? Just to prove to you I'm right."

Fortunately, the city limits of Austin came into view.

And I sighed with relief. "Okay."

I pulled up in front of the Chester mansion. Justin remained motionless. "It hasn't changed much." He looked around at me. The expression on his face reminded me of a frightened boy heading for the woodshed and a date with a paddle. "Maybe we ought to go get something to eat first. What do you think, Tony?"

"No. Your family's been waiting for you, Justin. They're eager to see you."

Clearing his throat nervously, he mumbled, "Would you mind very much going inside with me, Tony?"

His request took me by surprise until I realized that after fifteen years, he was almost like a stranger in his own home. And even if his family did not treat him as such, he would feel that way.

With a grin, I laid a hand on his shoulder. "No problem, Justin. Let's get it done."

Halfway up the walk, the door flew open, and Tricia hurried out to meet him, tears running down her cheeks. She threw her arms around his neck and hugged him to her. "Oh, Justin, Justin. It's been so long."

Tentatively, he put his arms around her. "Hello, Tricia."

At that moment, Vanessa and Frank appeared in the open doorway. A wry grin played over Frank's lips, while Vanessa's eyebrows knit with impatience.

I slapped Justin on the back. "Here you are. Good luck."

Anxiously, he turned to me. "No, come on in, Tony. We'll get something to eat."

"No. It's your family. You'll want to talk about your plans. Look me up later. We can shoot the breeze."

He looked at me wistfully, his eyes begging me to stay.

You've no idea how many times since that moment I've awakened at night and wished I'd gone inside with him.

I talked to Justin one more time, but that day was the last time I saw him alive.

Chapter Seven

The next couple of weeks flew by.

Two days before Beatrice Morrison's annual winter fete for Austin's upper crust, Janice called with the welcome news that her aunt didn't need the gumbo after all. She was having a hundred and fifty pounds of herb-and-chipotle–crusted flounder with smoked-mushroom aioli and gingered vegetables flown in from New Orleans. I had no idea what it was, but I didn't argue.

Just after we hung up, I got a call from Justin Chester in Elysian Hills. "I've got it, Tony. I told you I would, and now I have it."

I frowned. "What?"

"Proof of the spaceship."

My first thought was that the ten million had driven him over the edge. And, as he explained, I began to believe I was right. "My metal detectors turned up a lot of items on the hill where the ship crashed. But one piece of metal that I found

52

while digging did not set off the metal detector. I haven't had it tested yet, but if it didn't set off the detector, then it has to be something unusual." He paused and in a hushed tone added, "It has hieroglyphics on it, like the stories said." Before I could respond, he continued. "And something else about this metal. It's thin, and you can crush it into a ball, and then guess what it does?"

My guesses would have ranged from "fall to the ground" to "remain crushed in a ball," but I refrained from the wisecracks. Instead, I noncommittally replied, "Beats me."

In a tone of awe and wonder, he replied, "When you lay it down, it unfolds. Out flat. And there's no sign of any creases." He paused, then repeated himself. "Fold it into quarters, lay it down, and it unfolds itself."

Now, that was hard to believe. "You haven't been drinking, have you, Justin?" I was half joking and half serious and half intrigued, although a few stiff drinks seemed to be the only logical explanation for the phenomenon he was claiming.

"Can't stand booze anymore, Tony. Not even beer. I get sick when I drink."

I had no idea what to say next. So that's what I said. "So, what's next?"

"Next I'm going find the alien's grave. I've looked through old records and talked to a lot of the old-timers whose folks were alive when it happened. I've got a good idea where to look in the cemetery. About fifty yards from the street marker, there used to be an old oak. White oak, I think. It's gone, but I think I can find where it was. He was supposed to be buried around there somewhere."

I rolled my eyes and whistled softly. "Well, good luck.

Keep me posted." I didn't really mean it. I just wanted to get off the line.

A few days later, when I learned he was dead, a strange sense of guilt washed over me.

Why I felt guilty, I'm not sure. Maybe it was because I thought Justin was foolish to follow such a ludicrous pursuit. Or maybe it was because he had trusted me, and I didn't believe him.

Whatever the reason, I owed the gentle man my presence at his funeral. He was a likeable human being who had troubled no one and gone out of his way to help others.

The day of Justin's funeral dawned cold and drab with a sharp wind from the north.

Roth Funeral Home conducted the service, a small affair attended by immediate family and a handful of friends and acquaintances.

To my surprise, when I entered the nave, I spotted an ornate urn on a pedestal at the front of the room. Justin Chester had been cremated.

After the brief service, Tricia Chester, wearing a black hat and dress, stopped me outside the funeral home. "Thank you for coming, Tony. Justin would have wanted you to be here. He thought the world of you."

Ears burning, I nodded and mumbled, "It's a shame. He had a lot of life ahead of him."

She blinked back the tears welling in her eyes. "The family and friends are gathering at the house." She laid a hand on my arm. "I'd like for you to come if you don't mind."

Death is a natural part of life. At the moment of our birth, we begin dying. I've never had any trouble facing the specter of death. Sure, there were times that death hurt more than others, but it is the final act for each of us on this earth.

On the other hand, I was always uncomfortable at a gathering after a funeral, although it was a common practice. Except for family, I always begged off.

Tricia must have seen the reticence in my face, for she lowered her voice and whispered urgently, "I must talk to you, Tony. I don't believe Justin's death was an accident."

That was enough said.

The crowd in the dayroom at the mansion was twice the size of the one at the funeral. The mood was subdued, but from the soft laughter and furtive smiles, I had the feeling that Justin Chester was the last thing on their minds.

Like a lord overseeing his realm, Frank Chester, with his wife on his arm, made his way around the room, greeting all with a somber look and a brief handshake.

When he reached me, he nodded and took my hand. He introduced me to his wife, Judith. Now, I've had the look of disdain fixed on me more times than I can count by Beatrice Morrison, my on-again, off-again significant other's aunt, who is the queen of the condescending eye.

Let me tell you, Judith Chester could match Beatrice condescending eye for condescending eye.

I nodded to her. "Pleased to meet you, Mrs. Chester."

A pained smile cracked her perfectly painted lips.

Frank spoke up, his voice resonating with patronizing gratitude. "Thank you for all you did for us, Mr. Boudreaux. At least we had the opportunity to spend some time with our brother."

And the lordly couple moved on.

Across the room, Tricia caught my eye and cut hers to the large veranda beyond the glass doors.

Pausing at the buffet, I skipped the cocktails and placed a couple of tiny sandwiches on a delicate china plate and went out to the veranda, halting at the three-foot brick wall around its perimeter. Beyond lay the gray waters of Lake Travis far below. I shivered as the December wind cut through my jacket.

Moments later, Tricia came to stand by my side. "Thank you for coming, Tony." She gestured to the lake, as if pointing out some of the sights. "I didn't know who else to call, but I think someone deliberately killed Justin, or had him killed."

I resisted the impulse to look at her. Instead, I played her game. "Just what happened?"

"Car wreck. The sheriff at Elysian Hills said the justice of the peace declared Justin was drunk when he lost control of his pickup. He ran into a tree, and the pickup rolled down the side of a hill into a creek."

A tiny frown knit my brow. Gus Perry was the sheriff, I remembered. He had denied knowing Justin, the very man on whom he had run a criminal check at the request of the elementary school principal, Georgiana Irvin, some months earlier. I nibbled at the sandwich and grimaced. Just my luck, pimento cheese. I hated pimento cheese. You'd think rich folks would at least have a slice of ham in there. Of course, maybe that's one reason they have so much money. "I didn't think Justin drank anymore."

For several seconds, Tricia remained silent. Then, in a soft, strained voice, she replied, "He doesn't—I mean, didn't. But that isn't all. Before he went back to that little town, uh—"

"Elysian Hills."

"Yes, Elysian Hills. We probated Father's will."

Now I couldn't resist looking around at her, a puzzled frown on my face. Through the window of the dayroom, I spotted Frank Chester looking on. I forced a laugh. "I guess you know we're being watched."

"I know." She hesitated. "Can we meet later? Say ten o'clock at the County Line Barbeque?"

Holding my smile, I nodded. "You know the place, huh?"

She nodded. "Surprised?"

I chuckled. "It isn't exactly a hangout for the rich and famous."

She blushed. "I'm not the rich and famous. So, will you?"

"Sure."

"And please," she added, her voice pleading, "be careful. I think my sister has someone following me."

I frowned. "Why?"

She chewed on her bottom lip. "I'm not sure, but I think that maybe my brother or sister might be the one who had Justin murdered."

Chapter Eight

"**W**hoeeeee, boy," I muttered when I climbed into my Silverado pickup. "What have you gotten yourself into now, Tony?"

In the hills west of Austin, the County Line Barbeque on Bee Tree Road is a rustic establishment that unquestionably serves the most mouthwatering, juiciest barbeque in all the South with the exception of that cooked by my Uncle Patric Thibodeaux over in Louisiana in the famed chest freezer he converted to a pit.

At first I was surprised that Tricia Chester had picked the County Line. The ambiance of the place didn't fit in with anyone's idea of haute cuisine or the grand atmosphere of the *Michelin Guide* restaurants she likely patronized.

She would be as out of place there as common sense is in the hallowed halls of Congress.

And then I realized that a venue like the County Line

was the last place anyone would guess she had gone. As far as her being followed, I'd find out soon enough.

Esther Carman, the restaurant owner, and I have known each other for years. Though she is a decade or so my senior, she doesn't look it. She wears western jeans and western shirts, and I have yet to see one of those little barrel-racing fillies on the circuit who does as much justice to her gaudy outfit as she.

After a few years, Esther gave me a parking spot out back. I entered through the kitchen. I was such a familiar face, no one paid me any attention.

That night, I arrived an hour early and parked in my usual spot. Esther frowned when I requested a table in the rear, the lovers' section behind the fake shrubbery. "Client tonight, Tony?"

"I'm not sure. We just don't want to be disturbed."

She grinned and winked at me.

"Come on, Esther. Nothing like that."

Nodding emphatically, she laughed. "I'll bet."

I pulled my hand back playfully as if I were going to swat her on her derriere. She wagged a finger at me. I laughed. "I'll be outside. Have the waiter show her to my table."

The smile faded from her face. "Serious business, huh?"

"I hope not."

Outside, I eased into the pine and cedar surrounding the restaurant. The night air carried a chill. I pulled my tweed jacket about me as I found a spot where I could view the parking lot. If Tricia was indeed being followed, I wanted to get a look at him—or her.

Time dragged.

A dozen more vehicles pulled in. One of them, a black Ford Taurus, deliberately backed into a spot in the last lane despite several empty slots closer to the restaurant entrance. I waited for the driver to emerge from the vehicle, but he remained inside.

Fifteen minutes before the hour, a nondescript Honda Accord pulled into the crowded lot, parking two lanes from the door. A woman slipped out.

As she passed under a security light, I saw she wore a light Windbreaker over dark slacks. I didn't recognize her until I caught her profile in the open doorway of the restaurant.

I glanced back at the black Ford. The driver remained behind the wheel.

As soon as Tricia closed the door, a man bundled in a topcoat slipped out of the Ford Taurus. His hat was pulled down over his eyes as he strode for the restaurant.

Just as he passed under the security light, I gave a shrill whistle. He froze and looked around.

My jaw dropped open. It was Bulldog Face—the same guy I had spotted back on the San Antonio Riverwalk. What the dickens was going on?

For several moments he studied the dark forest of pine and cedar, then, with a shake of his head, went into the restaurant.

I pondered the situation. He had arrived earlier than Tricia. That meant someone had told him where she was going. And she was the only one who could have provided that information. Unless dear Brother and Sister had bugged the veranda, and even as skeptical as I had become regarding human nature, that was a stretch.

Slipping to the rear of the County Line, I came in through the kitchen.

Tricia looked up when she spotted me. "I thought maybe you'd changed your mind."

"Well, not until I hear what's going on." I eyed her plain clothes. "I almost didn't recognize you."

Her cheeks colored. "I hope you don't think I'm some foolish schoolgirl overreacting, but I didn't want anyone to know I was here."

"Did you mention coming to anyone?"

She frowned. "No. Well, only to my maid, in case she needed to get in touch with me. Why?"

"Just asking." I glanced past the fake plants but failed to spot my ugly friend.

Neither of us was hungry, but I ordered a pitcher of beer, in which Tricia gladly joined me.

I licked the foam from my lips. "So, tell me. What's going on?"

"Like I said today, Justin didn't drink anymore. Somebody lied. We can't do an autopsy, because he'd already been cremated before I thought." Her face twisted in anguish. "In my heart, I know he was murdered."

Resting my elbows on the table, I leaned forward. "You mentioned your brother and sister."

"Yes. When Father's will was probated, we learned that although each of us received ten million from his personal estate, upon the passing of any sibling, his or her share is to be divided among the others. If he or she had married, half of his or her inheritance would go to the spouse before the division."

I arched an eyebrow. It appeared the old man still wanted

to control his children even from the grave. "What about Frank's wife, Judith? Seems to me she'd object to that."

"She did until Frank pointed out that all the rest of his holdings would go to her."

"It's that much?"

She smiled at the skepticism in my tone. "Oh, yes. Frank was a partner with Father. They were more like brothers than father and son. That's another thirty million."

Like brothers. That explained the first-name business. With a soft whistle, I leaned back and shook my head. Figures like that boggled my brain.

She continued. "I don't want to think that Vanessa or Frank could commit such a reprehensible act, but they are both greedy. I don't know why, because we've had money all our lives."

I suppressed the cynicism in me to keep from telling her that that was probably the reason. The more one has, the more one wants. It's called avarice.

"Sometimes," she continued, "I think they resented Justin because he didn't care about the money. I know Father was always puzzled about him. With the rest of us, Father used money to force us to do what he wanted, but he couldn't do that with Justin." She paused, and a sad smile played over her lips. "Poor Father. He never could figure out why Justin never touched any of the funds in the bank account Father set up for him."

Right then, I wished I had known Justin better. A young man's convictions have to be mighty firm to ignore a $25,000 bank account lying there waiting to be tapped. And then I realized that perhaps Justin was a little smarter than the others and was aware that while gold will get you through many gates, it won't get you through heaven's.

"Do you have any proof that either Vanessa or Frank was responsible?"

"No," she replied softly. She hesitated. "Except that I saw Vanessa talking to some man. I don't know what about, but he didn't look like the kind of individual that we associate with in our group—" She caught herself. Her face turned crimson. "I'm sorry, Tony. I'm being snobbish, and I don't mean to be."

I slurped my beer and deliberately drew the back of my hand across my lips. "Forget it, Tricia. I feel the same way about you rich people. Present company excepted, I don't like being around 'em. So maybe in my own way, I'm a snob."

She laughed. "But, you know, there is a big difference in a rich snob and a poor snob, present company excepted."

Then we both laughed.

I liked her, truly liked the woman. "So, what do you want from me?"

Her dark eyes studied me for several moments. She chewed on her bottom lip as she tried to make up her mind. Finally she spoke, her voice soft but firm. "I want you to find the truth."

"What about Frank and Vanessa?"

"Don't worry. I'll tell them. I won't say I suspect them, but I will inform them I've hired you and paid you with my money to return to Elysian Hills and take care of any of Justin's unfinished business."

"Unfinished business, huh? Why up there, if you suspect

your brother or sister? Besides, I can't investigate a murder. My boss would lose his license."

She arched a devious eyebrow. "I'll know you'll have work to do here—on them—but he died up there. Someone might know something. Besides, his belongings are still up there." She paused, and a sly smile played over her lips. "I'm no detective, but it seems to me, this winding up the unfinished business gives you an excuse to . . ." She hesitated, searching for the right word.

Although I figured she was stretching it by suggesting some sort of covert involvement in Elysian Hills, I grinned at her audacity. "Snoop," I suggested.

Tricia grinned.

I grinned back at her. "You surprise me."

A frown erased her crooked smile. "Oh?"

"Yeah. You're devious."

"I guess that comes from being rich."

I considered her offer. I'd liked Justin, and if someone had murdered him, I wanted to know. A little judicious snooping wouldn't hurt anything while I was in the process of "winding up his business." "You'll need to come by the office."

She smiled. "No problem."

I glanced over her shoulder at the crowd filling the restaurant. I had mentioned nothing of Bulldog Face, but now the time was right. "You saw the man Vanessa was talking to, right?"

"Yes."

Pushing back from the table, I said, "Come with me."

She frowned. "What?"

"Come on. I want to show you something."

She rose to follow but protested when I headed for the kitchen. "Just do as I say. Now, come on."

The kitchen staff ignored us. I rubbed the steam from a small window and peered through it. I spotted Bulldog Face seated in a booth by himself. "Look over there at the booths along the wall. That ugly one, sitting by himself—is he the one you saw?"

She stood on tiptoe and gasped. "Why, yes. That's him." She looked around at me in surprise. "How—How—"

Taking her arm, I led her back to the table. "Wait here. I'll be back in a few minutes, and then I'll tell you all about it."

Slipping out the back, I dug out the thirty-foot length of tow chain I carry in the toolbox in the back of my Silverado. Fumbling through the box, I found my supply of locks.

What I had in mind I'd seen in a movie years earlier, and I had always wanted to give it a try. Now was the perfect time. I felt like a mischievous teenager as I snaked through the parking lot to the black Ford on the last aisle. It took only a minute to loop the chain around its axles and lock the other end around a tall pine.

Before I left, I made a mental note of the license number.

I guessed Vanessa didn't want any surprises. That's why she'd put a tail on her own sister. But this would let the Bride of Frankenstein know that her little secret was out.

Tricia looked up hopefully when I returned. I held out my hand. "Let's go. I want to get you out of here." I dropped twenty bucks by the half-full pitcher of draft beer and, taking her by the hand, eased her from her chair.

"Now what?"

Glancing over my shoulder, I replied, "Obviously that joker is the tail your sister hired. He waited out there until you parked, then followed you in." I glanced at the front door. "Now, here's what you do. Get your keys and walk directly to your car. Get in, start it up, and get out of here. He'll follow."

"But what if he stops me?"

"He won't. And, trust me, he won't follow you more than a few feet."

I could see the apprehension in her face. I patted her hand. "I know what I'm doing. Now, go. And if your sister should mention anything about tonight, play dumb."

A crooked grin played over her lips. "That won't be hard. I've got no idea what's going on."

Hurrying out the rear and around to the back lane, I watched as Tricia started her car. Seconds after the lights flashed on, the restaurant door burst open, and Bulldog Face came running across the lot.

By now, Tricia had exited the parking area and was pulling onto the highway below.

The Ford's engine roared to life, and the car shot forward. In a shrill shriek of ripping metal, the howling automobile jerked to a sudden halt, and its rear end shot up into the air and then crashed to the gravel, raising a cloud of dust.

I grinned and muttered. "Thanks, *American Graffiti*!"

Chapter Nine

During the drive back to my apartment on Payton-Gin Road, I went back over what little information I had. First, Vanessa Chester had hired Bulldog Face to tail her sister. Why? Obviously, to see what she was up to.

No question she had hired him to find Justin, but why, after she insisted she would spend none of her money on the effort to locate her brother?

I had spotted him in San Antonio three times. He had to have been tailing me. Someone had entered my room. Could he be the one? But if so, he'd learned nothing. From what Bones had said, Bulldog Face never found the Grasshoppers, so he couldn't have discovered Elysian Hills.

So, if he were responsible for Justin's death, the only way he could have learned of the small community was from Vanessa, and only after Justin returned to Austin, which made her a conspirator.

Motive? Plenty of that. Hey, ten million is motive enough

to check out just about anyone, except perhaps the Pope. And then—well, I won't say any more.

That night, I dreamed about Justin and the spaceship. I saw him crumpling the piece of aircraft skin, and then, as if by magic, it unfolded itself.

That's when A.B. jumped onto the bed and awakened me.

As long as I can remember, I've had pets around. As I grew older, they became more of a chore, but I was forced to keep them. Have you ever tried to find a home for a cat? What about a brain-damaged Albino Barb exotic fish?

I've had them all, and now it was A.B. He had it made. And the little guy couldn't argue that. All had been right with his world ever since that day I plucked him from the grasp of two swamp Neanderthals who were planning on running a 12/0 shark hook through him for alligator bait. That's how he came up with that moniker, A.B.

Down at the office the next day, I briefed Marty on the situation. When Tricia arrived, I reminded her that she was not hiring us to investigate Justin's death but to gather his belongings and talk to his friends, both in Austin and Elysian Hills.

She glanced warily at Marty.

I winked at her. "I told him everything."

She seemed to relax. "Good. I told the sheriff up there we were sending someone to gather Justin's possessions and talk to the people he worked with. He's expecting you."

Once again I took care to explain that since the body had been cremated, we could not prove Justin had not been drinking. The justice of the peace's report would stand.

"I understand, but—" She paused and glanced at Marty. "As I told Tony, I want to know, if for nothing else, for my own peace of mind. If my brother or sister is involved, then . . ." Her voice trailed off.

Marty shrugged. "We'll do you a good job, Miss Chester. Don't you worry."

After she left, I turned to Marty. "Must be a good feeling not to worry. Looks like I'm the only one worrying here."

Marty slapped me on the shoulder. "Stop it then, Tony. Look into the brother and sister here. Then get up there and pick up his junk. Talk to the people in town, then come on back and write up the report, and we bill her. Simple. Hey, the guy got drunk and killed himself. That's all there is to it."

I wondered how it felt to be so omniscient. "All right."

I didn't mention it to Tricia, for I could see no sense in upsetting her any further, but in any murder investigation, the first suspects are always family. I not only wanted to check out Frank and Vanessa, as she wanted, too, but also Tricia herself before returning to Elysian Hills, where I didn't expect to learn anything. In fact, I didn't plan on being there more than a few hours.

My first job, however, was to run a check on the license number of the goon tailing Tricia. It belonged to Lone Star Security, another PI office in Austin.

After that, it was a simple matter of going to Lone Star's Web site and pulling up its employees, but my man wasn't among them.

I gave Lone Star a call. Five minutes later I hung up and leaned back in my chair. The Ford had been stolen. That put the entire matter in a different light.

On impulse, I dialed Danny O'Banion. Austin's rumored

caporegime. Danny and I go way back to high school, where we got into a few jams together. He dropped out in the eleventh grade, and we lost touch. Next time I ran into him was at the annual UT-Oklahoma brawl in Dallas. We sipped from his silver flask, laughed a little, lied a lot, and then went our separate ways.

I endeared myself to his people when I saved them a bundle of cash—a big bundle. On two or three occasions over the last few years, he'd sent his soldiers to bail me out of untenable situations in which I had idiotically placed myself. Whenever I needed information about his side of the street, he had proven invaluable.

This time was no different.

After I described my man, Danny grunted. "The only one that ugly is Lester Taggart. They call him Bulldog. He's a freelance muscleman. For the right money, he'll do a hit, nice and clean." He paused. When he continued, there was a hint of concern in his voice. "Be careful around him, Tony. The guy's bananas. No telling what he'll do." He paused and added, "One thing about him, though—the guy is as loyal as a pet dog. He takes a job, he finishes it. That's why he's in demand."

I stared at the receiver after I hung up, wondering just how many rocks Vanessa Chester had had to turn over before finding this particular snake. I moved her to the top of my suspect list.

That night, I booted up my computer and went online with Eddie Dyson, my savior on more occasions than I could remember.

At one time Austin's resident stool pigeon, Eddie Dyson

had become a computer whiz and wildly successful entrepreneur.

I've always heard that all one must do to be successful in life is to find his niche. Well, instead of in sleazy bars and greasy money, Eddie discovered his niche for snitching in the bright glow of computers. Any information I couldn't find, he could. There were only two catches if you dealt with Eddie. First, you never asked him how he did it, and second, he only accepted VISA credit cards for payment.

I never asked Eddie why he only accepted VISA. Seems like any credit card would be sufficient, but, considering the value of his services, I never posed the question. As far as I was concerned, if he wanted to be paid in Japanese yen, I'd pack up a bushel and send it to him.

Failure was not in his vocabulary. His services did not come cheaply, but he produced. And in my business, usually the end is indeed worth the means.

I was hoping it would be this time. I wanted background information on all three of the Chesters.

Sometimes my boss, Marty, frustrates me, but he is an experienced PI, and his ever-present caution to "mistrust everyone" has proven more than once to be an unimpeachable tenet of our business.

The next day, just after lunch, Eddie responded to my queries.

Usually his information provides details that point me in the direction of the guilt of a particular individual, but this time, all three of the subjects had motives for wanting to see Justin dead.

Money.

I rolled my eyes. What else?

Frank, while sitting on about a $30,000,000 business, not counting his inheritance, was in hock up to twice that amount.

Vanessa Chester was down to her last hundred thousand, with bills three times that much coming due.

And not to leave Tricia Chester out, she not only was broke, but three banks were carrying her personal notes in the amount of $800,000.

Whistling softly, I shook my head. Old man Chester had kicked off just in time.

I dug deeply into the Chesters' backgrounds. I asked Danny to see what he could learn through his channels. He found nothing, which in turn just about convinced me that if any of the Chesters were involved in Justin's death, Vanessa was the most likely.

Taggart had not located Justin in Elysian Hills the first time, but Vanessa had known that Justin was returning to the hamlet. She could have sent Taggart after him.

I pointed out the flaws in my theory to myself. Vanessa never left Austin, and I was certain Taggart would have an ironclad alibi for his whereabouts at the time of Justin's death. Besides, why take a chance for only three million when you had just come into ten?

Obviously, avarice, greed, gluttony.

Talk about divine intervention. Well, not exactly divine. *Mobster* is probably a better adjective, for at that moment the telephone rang. It was Danny. "What day did you say that Chester dude got himself killed?"

"November 28. The pickup wrecked about eight or eight-thirty that night."

He grunted. "I thought that's what you had told me. Well, I'm afraid I've got some unpleasant news for you, Tony. Two of my boys were celebrating Red Davis' birthday at The Red Rooster down on Sixth Street that night. Our friend Taggart was there until closing time."

I felt as if someone had kicked me in the face. So much for my Vanessa theory. "You're certain?"

"Yep. These are two of my best boys. Hardly drink. If they say Taggart was there, he was there."

"Okay, Danny. Thanks. See you when I get back."

"Anytime. But look, you be careful up there. Maybe I ought to send one of my boys with you."

"Thanks, but no, thanks."

"I think I should. I got one of those feelings."

I laughed. "Probably gas. Thanks anyway."

He chuckled. "Probably."

To my frustration, I had been unable to find any ominous connection between the siblings and Justin. I had called every snitch, every goon I knew, and nothing was floating about. Who else would have a reason to kill him?

No one.

I was puzzled as to my next step. I felt I was overlooking something, but what?

The human brain is an amazing device of which only a small percentage is truly utilized. It assimilates and synthesizes in ways we have yet to comprehend. That capability was demonstrated to me that evening.

That night, December 7, I watched a documentary on the bombing of Pearl Harbor. According to the commentator, one of the tactical ploys of the Japanese attack was to hope that the Americans believed the incoming aircraft were their own.

That stuck with me. Their own. Then a crazy idea popped into my head.

"Maybe," I muttered, staring at the TV, "maybe the killer isn't from Austin, like Tricia thought, but from Elysian Hills." I knew I was reaching, but if Justin had been murdered, and if his brothers and sisters were not involved, then the answer had to be in Elysian Hills.

Closing my eyes and leaning back, I shook my head. "No. That's impossible." What in a small, backwoods community like Elysian Hills could precipitate murder?

Then another idea struck me. Why *couldn't* Justin have been drinking? When he talked to me, he was excited about some of the evidence he had uncovered. Why couldn't he have had his own little celebration despite his feelings about drinking? Hey, we all backslide.

Next morning, I called Tricia to inform her I was pulling out for Elysian Hills to pick up her brother's belongings. I added, "It looks like your fears concerning your brother and sister are unfounded."

In a puzzled tone, she replied, "But what about the man at the barbeque place?"

I had expected her to ask that question, so I told her what I surmised. "Obviously, Vanessa wanted to know what you were up to. His name is Taggart, by the way." I paused, then continued. "At first, I thought there might be a connection, but I have definite proof that Taggart was in Austin the night your brother had his accident. He could not have been in Elysian Hills."

She paused, then replied, "I'm really confused now."

With a chuckle, I replied, "Maybe you ought to ask Vanessa to straighten you out."

To my surprise, Tricia replied, "I might do that very thing, although I still don't trust her. I still don't know how she found out I was meeting you at the County Line."

I chuckled. "Ask your maid."

Chapter Ten

The weather grew colder the farther north I drove.

During the drive to Elysian Hills, I replayed all I knew about Justin Chester. In a way, I felt guilty. If I had never located him, the poor guy might still be alive. From what I had seen, he was as content as a new kitten with his janitor's salary and his room behind the museum and his mission to discover the spaceman. I couldn't help remembering Narelle's wisecrack at the bar back in San Antonio. *"Some guys have all the luck."*

Some luck!

By the time I reached the small community, I had convinced myself—probably because that's what I wanted to believe—that the wreck was exactly what the justice of the peace had ruled, an accident caused by an inebriated driver. But that posed another question. Was Justin's discovery exciting enough to coax him into taking a drink, even though, according to him, alcohol made him sick? I shook my head. It was times like this that I wished I were smarter.

Despite the sunshine, the day was brittle cold with a chilling wind sweeping down across the prairie, cutting clean to the bone.

Sheriff Gus Perry looked up at me in surprise when I entered. He snorted. "Heard you was coming up." He grinned apologetically. "Sorry I wasn't more help when you first got here. I didn't recognize the picture, and I'd never heard his name. Most around here called him UFO."

I shrugged. "No problem. I'm here to pick up Justin's belongings, all his stuff."

He pushed back from his desk. "Then I got something for you." Opening the top drawer of the file cabinet behind his desk, he pulled out a small accordion folder and handed it to me. "This is all the stuff that was in his pickup." A crooked grin played over his rugged face. "I left the empty bourbon bottle on the floorboard. Didn't figure the family would appreciate it." He hooked a thumb over his shoulder. "The rest of his stuff is out at his room at the museum." He shook his head and grunted. "Living in a dump like that after coming into all that money. It don't make sense."

I could see no reason to try to explain Justin Chester to the sheriff. I agreed. "No sense at all, Sheriff. Did anyone see the wreck?" He frowned, and I explained. "The report you and the JP filed was very thorough." A smug grin played over his lips as I added, "His family appreciated it, but they asked me to see if I could find out anything else. You know, maybe who found him, that sort of thing. Personally, I don't think I would want to know, but—" I gave an indifferent shrug. "But you know how it is."

I suppressed a sigh of relief when he nodded.

"Yeah? Well, if that's what they want. It was old Buck Ford who called me. I'd gone home a couple hours early to tend to a sick heifer. He's the one what found Chester. Seems the man lost control of his old Ford pickup on Cemetery Road. Bounced off a tree and rolled down into a gully. The JP, George McDaniel—he runs the feed store up the road—well, he said Chester was drunk." He wrinkled his nose. "Smelled like a still in the pickup."

"He, uh, have any sobriety tests run?"

Perry shrugged. "No need. It was obvious."

I had to remind myself I was in the middle of good-old-boy country. They approached just about everything much more casually than did the boys in Austin. "This Buck Ford. He live close by?"

The sheriff hesitated a moment before replying. "First road past Hooker's. Take a right. His is the first place you see, about half a mile up." He paused and chuckled. "It's the only place on the road."

"Thanks." I paused and nodded in the direction of the UFO museum. "Justin was pretty deep into that UFO stuff, wasn't he?"

Perry eyed me suspiciously. "Like I told you before. That's all it was, just stuff and nonsense. It was all one big hoax. Everyone knows it." He rose and headed for the coffeepot. "Care for a cup? This time of day, I need a pick-me-up."

"Might as well."

He set out an extra cup. "Sugar and cream if you want

it." He poured two cups and continued. "I didn't know UFO—I mean, Chester—all that good. He was a strange bird, but maybe if he hadn't took that UFO nonsense so serious, he'd still be alive. I tried to convince him, but he paid me no mind."

The coffee was strong, almost as strong as the brew served back in Louisiana. "Did he ever tell you what he was looking for?"

"Some. He was convinced the hoax really happened. That it wasn't no hoax."

I knew the story, but the sheriff seemed to be loosening up. I cleared my throat. "I never heard it all, just the bits and pieces Justin told me on the way back to Austin last month."

He sipped his coffee and fished a cigarette from his pocket. He offered me one, but I declined. "Gave it up years ago."

Perry grinned ruefully, the freckles on his face all scrunching together. "Wish I could. Bad for a feller." He touched a match to his cigarette. "Nothing to the story. Like I said, it's one big hoax." He chuckled. "Even got some newspaper coverage. But that's all it was, just a hoax."

"Newspaper coverage, huh?"

He nodded emphatically. "Yep. *Dallas Morning Telegram*. Got a bunch of write-ups for a month or so until it sort of died out. About fifty years later, it popped up again. Well, the mayor at the time, Jim Bob Houston, whose pa had been one of them what made it all up to begin with, wrote the Dallas paper a letter telling them about the hoax. In fact, Mabel Hooker over at the gas station has the letter framed on her wall. It's right next to the original newspaper article. We get a big kick out of them."

"I'd like to see them."

"Like I said, they're right on the wall at Mabel's."

I sipped my coffee. "Justin called me after he got back here. Said he'd been exploring. He find anything?"

Perry pursed his lips and with a wry grin replied, "I don't know how. Ain't nothing out there to find."

For some reason, I said nothing of the piece of aircraft skin Justin had mentioned. I wasn't sure why. Maybe I didn't want to appear gullible. Or maybe I didn't want the sheriff to know as much as I knew. "You lived around here long, Sheriff?"

"All my life." He dropped the cigarette butt onto the wood floor and ground it under his heel. "My pa and grandpa before me. That's how I know it was all a hoax. When I was six or seven, Grandpa Joe told me all about it. He said the townsfolk got a good laugh until so many city people came in, running over plowed fields, putting the cows off their milk, and in general upsetting everything."

Setting my empty cup next to the pot, I thanked him. "Enjoyed our visit, Sheriff Perry. Now, who do I need to see about getting into Justin's room?"

He pointed in the direction of the museum. "The big red-brick house on the hill behind the museum. "Marvin Lewis lives there. He's got a few sections of land out back. He owns the museum. Used to be a state senator way back."

After leaving the sheriff's office, I pulled up in front of the gas pumps at Hooker's. I don't know how old the pumps were, but they were at least a couple of generations before credit-card pumps. The frigid north wind was merciless. I shivered as I filled the tank.

Across the road, an old man in baggy clothes, a battered fedora pulled down over his ears, and his coat collar pulled up about his neck, shuffled along the shoulder kind of sideways, his back to the biting wind, his worn shoes kicking up puffs of dust. The wind whipped his jacket around him. After I topped off the tanks, I went inside to pay.

I groaned in pleasure at the warmth inside. Mabel Hooker stood behind the register, garbed in a bright red sweat suit, her gray hair pulled back into a severe bun. She recognized me immediately. A warm smile leaped to her ruddy face. "Well, what brings you back here?"

After I told her, she shook her head. "I didn't know the man, but those what did said he was a real gentleman. Real shame."

"Yeah. By the way, the sheriff was telling me about the UFO business your little town is known for." I glanced out the front window. The old man turned down a narrow road heading south.

She laughed. "I suppose ever'place has to be famous for something. Yeah. Big story back then. Every once in a while even now it crops up, and we have a few curious sightseers come through. That's about the only time old Marvin unlocks the museum, despite what his sign says."

"Sheriff said you had a letter and a newspaper article about it on your wall," I said, glancing around the store.

She indicated two framed documents on the wall beside the front door. "That's them right there. The mayor back then, Jim Bob Houston, wrote the letter to the editor of the Dallas newspaper that had printed a story about the spaceship. Seems Jim Bob's granddaddy, Jake, was one of them what cooked up the scheme. The story I always heard was that Elysian Hills was dying, so one day when Jake was drinking with A. B. Smith and Howard Nash, both town councilmen, they cooked up the scheme. Way I hear, there was a big commotion for a few months."

I laughed. "I can imagine."

Wandering over to the framed documents, I read them.

The article from the *Dallas Morning Telegram* was dated April 19, 1897.

. . . About six o'clock this morning the early risers of Elysian Hills were astonished by the sudden appearance of an unusual airship. Evidently some of the machinery was out of order, for it was making a speed of only ten or twelve miles an hour and gradually settling toward the Earth. It sailed over the public square, and when it reached the north part of town, it collided with the tower of Judge Lewis' windmill and went into pieces with a terrific explosion, scattering debris over several acres of ground, wrecking the windmill and water tank and destroying the judge's flower garden. The pilot of the ship is supposed to have been the only one aboard, and, while his remains were badly disfigured, enough of them were picked up to show that he was not an inhabitant of this world.

I couldn't help chuckling when I finished the news article.

The second document, the mayor's letter, dated sixty years later, was on Elysian Hills letterhead and signed by the mayor.

November 16, 1957

George Wilson, Editor
Dallas Morning Telegram
1284 Main St.
Dallas, Texas

Dear Mr. Wilson,

Recently, your paper ran an article about the UFO in Elysian Hills in 1897. This letter is to inform you and your readers that the story was a hoax, perpetrated by three local citizens.

As mayor of our beautiful city, I feel I am obligated to notify you of this matter. I regret any problems our citizens might have created.

Respectfully,
Jim Bob Houston, Mayor
Elysian Hills, Texas

Being an ex-English teacher, I raised an eyebrow in appreciation at the succinct letter. Mayor Jim Bob Houston must have had a pretty fair secretary.

From behind, Mabel laughed. "Now you see what we're so famous for."

Turning back, I chuckled. "Makes for a good story. This Jim Bob Houston, he still around?"

A sly grin played over her ruddy face. "Reckon he's another one of them mysteries all towns got."

Her reply piqued my curiosity. "Oh? What sort of mystery?"

She chuckled and began restocking the cigarettes above the register. "About thirty years later, around eighty-six, he just up and sold out. Moved up north. Never told a soul. I was about—let's see . . ." She hesitated and gave me a sly grin. "Well, how old I was ain't no matter."

I chuckled.

She continued. "I always figured it was kinda strange. Should have expected something, I guess. His wife had left him a couple years before. I suppose he was ready to move on. He never had no children. All he had was five or six sections of land. What with cattle and a few oil wells getting ready to come in, it brought him a pretty penny, so he never was hurting for money. Heard later, he set up some trusts for needy folks up north around Chicago." She shrugged. "Don't know for certain, but that's the word what come back."

I thought nothing of her remarks at the time. "This Marvin Lewis who owns the museum. Any kin to the judge in the article?"

"His grandson. In fact, Marvin is the one who bought out Jim Bob. He sold part of Jim Bob's acreage to the sheriff and Buck Ford."

I glanced out the window at the museum east of us. It was built into the side of a hill like the old dugouts of a couple hundred years back. "Not much business over there, huh? Why does he keep it open if the whole thing was a hoax?"

Mabel came to stand beside me, peering out the window. "Probably because Marv don't believe it was a hoax."

Chapter Eleven

I looked down at her in surprise. "You mean . . ."

She arched an eyebrow. That's when I noticed that her eyes were almost the color of turquoise. She must have been a knockout when she was younger. Even now, take her hair out of the bun and put her in something besides baggy red sweats, and she would make a striking picture. "Yep. Marv claims his grandpa told him that there was a space pilot, just like the story says. They buried him in an unmarked grave at the cemetery so no one could dig him up."

"So, with Justin Chester living in a room at the back of the museum, he and Marvin Lewis must have hit it off. I mean, with both of them believing in the UFO business."

Mabel laughed. "You got that right. Two peas in a pod. I don't know about Justin, but Marv . . ." She hesitated, searching for the right words. "Marv has always been one of those what never fit in. It's of his own choosing, of course. He never ran with the crowd, always saw things different.

85

Sometimes I thought he was being contrary just to be contrary. Someone call a color black, he'd call it red just to be different." She frowned up at me. "Know what I mean?"

A wry grin twisted my lips. I knew the kind. Those who, Thoreau wrote in *Walden,* hear a different drummer. "Exactly."

She hastened to add, "Now, Marv's a good man. Contrary he is, but that contrariness sure helped us out when he represented us in the state legislature back in the eighties."

I arched an eyebrow. "Oh?"

Gesturing to the oil wells in the pasture across the highway, she explained, "There was some problem with mineral rights ownership back then. The state insisted it belonged to them because the mineral rights were not included in the Spanish land grants or some falderal like that, but Marv straightened them out." She chuckled. "Good and proper, so around here, we just kind of overlook his peculiarities. If he wants to believe in UFOs, let him."

I studied the museum. "How old is that place?"

She grunted. "It's been there as long as I can remember. When I was a kid, we played on it. The roof had caved in. All that was standing were the walls. Then, about fifty years ago, Marv roofed it."

"What kind of stuff does he have in there?"

She snorted. "Junk. Pieces he claims came from the spaceship, but they're just pieces of old busted up farm machinery. Every once m a while it draws some poor sucker tourist in."

"Were you here the night Justin wrecked?"

"Just finished cleaning up. About eight or so, maybe a little after. Buck Ford come banging on my door something fierce for the phone so he could call the sheriff. His cell battery was dead." She chuckled. "I was surprised he got Gus."

I frowned at her. "Oh? Why's that?"

"Gus almost didn't have time to get home. He'd come by here not five minutes before. He's got a place several miles out."

"Did you go down to the wreck?"

"Heavens, no. I see enough bad things on TV. I got no interest in seeing the real thing."

"Where did the accident happen?"

"See that gravel road on the other side of the highway there, just across from the Christian church? That's Cemetery Road. About a mile down it makes a sharp *S* curve before reaching the old bridge. Justin went through the fence just before the curve and hit a big oak before going into the creek."

I made a mental note to drive by the scene so I could describe it to the family in case one of them asked.

The country around Elysian Hills is fairly open and rolling—like many Texans brag, nothing but wide-open spaces. And far to the west of those wide-open spaces, the sun dropped below the horizon. With the coming night, the temperature began to fall. The weatherman had forecast a light freeze.

My stomach growled. I was ready for a hot meal and a warm bed. I'd visit Buck Ford first thing in the morning. "Where's the nearest motel around here?"

Pointing east, she replied, "Bunch of them on I-35 at Reuben. About ten miles. The Bucket Inn Motel is the cleanest."

Having grown up on a farm outside of Church Point, I

was familiar with the eerie loneliness of vast spaces. Even during daylight, the overwhelming sense of solitude seemed ready to engulf you, and the gray of dusk settling over hundreds of square miles of desolate prairies exacerbated the feeling.

So when I spotted the beckoning lights of the truck stops and motels along I-35, a grin came to my face.

After checking in, I enjoyed a thick steak downstairs at the Bucket Inn restaurant.

Satisfied after a filling meal, I returned to my room to update my note cards for the day. Tomorrow, I planned to visit Buck Ford and Marvin Lewis.

I paused as I studied the cards I'd written concerning my conversation with the sheriff. I still couldn't understand how Sheriff Paley could run a criminal check on Justin and not remember the guy's name.

There was a nip in the air next morning.

Just after eight, I headed for Elysian Hills. I had risen early, enjoyed a breakfast of sausage, pancakes soaked with butter and syrup, and coffee—what some Cajuns considered a heart-healthy breakfast.

Before I pulled out, on impulse I purchased a copy of *The Reuben Journal* and scanned it for local news that meant nothing to me.

The narrow macadam road between Elysian Hills and I-35 meandered over the hills and through the valleys. To my surprise, there was more traffic than I would have guessed: pickups from the bedroom communities commuting to work; cattle trucks hauling beef to market; and oil tankers carrying freshly pumped oil to refineries.

America on the move.

The sun was at my back. I had to adjust the rearview mirror to keep it from blinding me.

I topped a hill, and my eyes popped open when I stared into the menacing grill of a giant Peterbilt eighteen-wheeler taking his half of the road right down the middle. I jerked onto the shoulder, struggling to slow the pickup and maintain control of the vehicle.

I finally braked to a halt off the road and for several moments sat staring in relief at the dash in front of me. "Good thing you saw him, Tony," I muttered. I glanced in the rearview, squinting into the sunlight, but the truck had disappeared over the crest of the hill.

All I could figure was that the sun had blinded the driver.

Buck Ford pumped oil and fattened cattle. A railroad spur ran up to his place, terminating inside a large metal barn. On either side of the spur sprawled several feed pens for beef. Half of them were filled with bawling cows. The smell smacked me full in the face.

As I turned into the drive, I had to pull over for a loaded cattle truck to pass. I couldn't help wondering if the truck that had run me off the road was one of Ford's.

I stopped at the office, which was a separate building from the white brick house. An older woman in western garb informed me that Buck was out at the barn.

Parking in front of the massive barn, I stepped out and tugged my tweed jacket about me. The air was crisp, and my breath frosted over. I whistled softly when I stepped through the open doors. It was huge, wide-open, and cold. You could fit a football field in it with room to spare. At one end of a raised platform, feed trucks were lined up, dumping their loads into large hoppers along the bottom of which ran conveyer belts with partitioned chambers carrying feed from the barn to the holding pens.

I spotted a small group of men in western hats and the requisite western regalia standing around a dozen bales of hay. Behind them, a propane burner poured warm air into the barn. They looked around as I approached. I nodded. "Morning. I'm looking for Buck Ford."

Three of the group looked at the fourth man.

"That's me," said the fourth one. Buck Ford was about my height, five-ten, but he outweighed me by seventy-five pounds, most of it in the watermelon belly pushing his heavy coat aside and draping over his silver-dollar belt buckle. His western shirt was stretched so tight over his stomach that I couldn't figure out how the little pearl buttons remained snapped.

I offered my hand and introduced myself. Briefly, I told him the purpose of my visit. "Sheriff Perry told me you found the wreck."

Ford ran the tip of his tongue behind his bottom lip, moving around his wad of snuff. "Yep. Coming back from one of my pastures out south. It was getting dark when I hit the bridge. If I hadn't been looking, I wouldn't have seen it. That's how dark it was. The old truck was brown."

One of the three spoke up. "I didn't know you found the wreck, Buck. You never said nothing about it."

Buck snorted and loosed a brown stream of tobacco onto the sandy floor. He reached for the twine banding a bale of hay and fumbled in his pocket. "Nothing to talk about. Chester was dead when I got down there. Started to strike a match to see, but gas was everywhere. I went back to my truck for a flashlight. Blood all over the place. Run all down his ears and neck." He jerked his hand from his pocket and muttered a sharp curse. "Lost that knife again."

"Here." I handed him mine, an old Case with the shield missing on the handle. "What did the pickup do, just go straight down into the creek?"

The other three moved a step closer, curious.

Buck cut the twine. He glanced at me and grinned. "Sharp."

"My grandpa would kick my tail if it wasn't."

He chuckled and tossed pieces of the bale onto the conveyor as he continued. "Chester must have bounced off the tree, then banged over the rocks until he slid nose first down into the creek." He paused and cut another bale free. "You boys know how steep it is there, where the creek bends just before the old bridge. I caught a glimpse of the pickup. I didn't recognize it, but I did Mr. Chester when I found him. He was facedown on the steering wheel, strapped in by his seat belt and deader than five-day-old roadkill. Must've slammed his head into the steering wheel mighty hard."

A thought struck me. "Had you ever met Justin Chester?"

"Nope."

As we talked, he cut the remainder of the bales.

My next question was how he knew it was Justin. If he'd banged his head on the wheel, then blood would have run down his forehead and covered his face. "How'd you know it wasn't someone else?"

He gave me an odd look. "I'd seen him around. Like I said, never met him, but I'd seen him around." He looked at the knife before folding it. "Old, huh?"

"Yep. My grandfather gave it to me."

He handed it to me. "Those Cases never wear out."

I agreed, then, dragging the fingers of my free hand from my forehead down to my chin, asked, "Wasn't his face covered with blood?"

Impatiently, he replied, running a single finger behind each ear and down his cheeks. "Like I just told you, the blood ran down his ears and neck. His face was gray looking." He shivered. "First dead man I'd ever seen outside a funeral."

The hair on the back of my neck tingled.

My brain was turning out more questions than answers. Only a contortionist could go headfirst down a steep embankment and not strike his forehead, unless he was already dead for several hours and rigor had set in, keeping the body stiff. And that might account for the coloring too.

"Anyway," he continued, "my cell phone was dead, so I went up to Hooker's and called the sheriff. He was waiting for me when I got back to the accident."

On impulse, I decided to take a look at the pickup. "Any idea where they hauled the pickup?"

"Nope. Newt Gibons down at the mechanic's shop can tell you. He has the local wrecker service. Probably to Johnson's, but I ain't certain. You need to ask Newt."

I thanked Buck and left, not realizing that I was walking into more trouble than I expected.

Chapter Twelve

My first hint of trouble came when I pulled back onto the highway and headed for Gibons' Automotive Shop. As I drew near Hooker's on my left, I spotted a familiar car, a white Cadillac convertible XLR. "Oh, no," I moaned, rolling my eyes and hoping it didn't have a 4.6 L V-8 engine and five-speed automatic. "Not Jack. Please, dear Lord, not Jack."

Reluctantly, I pulled into Hooker's and lowered the window. Even before I could climb out, I knew the good Lord had decided not to grant my pleas. Jack Edney came rolling out the door wearing a red Windbreaker, waving his short arms enthusiastically. "Hey, Tony. Hi there. Surprised?"

Surprised was not the word I would have selected. *Stunned, staggered,* or perhaps *shocked.* Any of the three would have fit my current state of mind better than *surprised.*

"What are you doing up here, Jack?"

The curt tone of my voice didn't faze him. With a grin as wide as the Colorado River, he replied. "Had to get away. It's crazy down there."

I arched an eyebrow. "Diane?"

He nodded. "Yeah. I need a break, Tony. That's the gospel." He stood there with a hangdog expression on his face. I studied him for several moments, remembering my despair, my melancholy the last few months I spent with Diane. And it wasn't all her fault. She was as uncomfortable with me. It's a shame marriages deteriorate into such a state. I suppose it's because neither wants to admit failure, and the situation goes from bad to worse. Finally, with a slow shake of my head, I mumbled, "Move your car around to the side of the store out of traffic, and get in."

When he clambered into the pickup cab, he brought along his ubiquitous ice chest. And unless I missed my guess, it was stocked with Budweiser. "I'm ready. Let's go." He grinned.

Newt Gibons' shop had three bays, all full with Buck Ford's trucks. A box-shaped portable propane heater sent out a stream of warm air swirling about the cavernous building. Jack waddled over in front of it and rubbed his hands together.

Gibons was a closemouthed little man about five-six and wearing baggy overalls. "Yep," he replied, wiping at the grease on his hands when I asked him if he'd towed the wrecked pickup.

"Mind telling me where you hauled it? His family wanted me to look through the glove compartment."

"Ain't nothing in it. Inside's covered with blood. Sheriff sent all the stuff in it to the family."

I shrugged indifferently. "I know it's a waste of time, but they're paying me to look again. You know how it is."

He jammed a greasy rag into his hip pocket. "Nope. Don't reckon I do."

At that moment, the back door creaked open. The old man I'd spotted ambling down the road the previous day when I was filling up with gas at Hooker's shuffled in. He paused, his rheumy eyes focused on Newt Gibons. "Got it cleaned up, Newt."

Newt glanced at me. "Just a minute." He fished a few dollars from his pocket and handed them to the old man. "Okay, Harlan. Come back next week, you hear?"

The old man nodded slowly.

After he left. Newt explained. "Old Harlan Barton. Town drunk. Lives out near the cemetery. Family lived out there since I don't know when. He's the last of the Bartons. Sold off everything except his shack. Cleans up oil cans and stuff out back for a few bucks."

I nodded. "So, where can I find it?"

For a moment, he didn't understand the question. Then he remembered. "You mean the pickup?"

"Yeah."

"Johnson's Salvage."

I waited for him to continue, but when it was obvious he had no intention of saying any more, I asked, "And where can I find Johnson's?"

He pointed northwest up the highway and snorted. "Everybody knows Johnson's."

With a patronizing grin, I replied, "Not me."

"Oh." He pointed west. "Well, Johnson's is about nine or ten miles up the highway there, just this side of Woodbine."

As we pulled onto the highway, I spotted Harlan Barton climbing into a pickup on the shoulder of the road. Buck Ford sat in the driver's seat.

During the drive to the wrecking yard, I called Tricia Chester back in Austin. I figured my cell signal might be too weak, but to my surprise, it was strong.

Tricia answered after several rings.

"Look, I don't mean to bring back unpleasant memories, but did you see Justin's remains before the cremation?"

"Yes. We all did. Why?"

Ignoring her question, I asked another. "Were there any marks on his forehead?"

Puzzled, she hesitated, then replied. "A tiny imprint, not even a bruise, about the size of a dime, but the skin wasn't broken. Why?"

"One more question. What funeral home did you use?"

Her tone grew impatient. "What's this all about, Tony? Why do you want to know all this?"

"I'll explain later. The funeral home? Which one was it?"

"Roth's. Why?"

"What's the number?"

Moments later, she read it off to me. "Now, what's going on? Have you learned something?"

Ahead loomed Johnson's Salvage. "Let me call you back tonight. I'm going to take a look at Justin's pickup."

"But—"

I punched off.

I started to call Roth's but on impulse dialed Danny O'Banion instead. I figured that getting information from the funeral home about Justin's facial trauma would be difficult for me, but Danny had hundreds of soldiers under him in every layer of Austin's populace.

"No sweat, Tony. I'll call you back. By the way, everything going okay?"

"Sure. No problem."

"You sure?" There was a note of suspicion in his voice.

"Positive."

"You sound funny. I'll send someone up there."

I laughed. "No. I'm fine. Talk to you later."

I pulled up in front of Johnson's and glanced at Jack. "Want to go in with me?"

"No. I'll sit out here and listen to the radio. He opened the ice chest and pulled out a Budweiser. He offered me one.

I chuckled. "At ten in the morning? Too early for me."

The day was warming quickly. Inside Johnson's office, an old gentleman in overalls and a plaid wool jacket looked up from behind the counter. I gave him a business card and explained my reason for being there.

He motioned for me to follow him. "Just out back."

I shook my head when I spotted the pickup. Typical Justin. Don't blow money. The truck was a brown 1990 Ford F-150 going on twenty years old. The impact had crumpled the front right fender, but that was all.

The old man running the place squirted a stream of tobacco juice onto the ground. "Truck's tore up pretty bad. Looks like a lot of front-end work."

I knew better, but I didn't respond as I went around to the

driver's door and peered inside. I opened the door and wrinkled my nose at the stench of gasoline, wondering how the sheriff could have smelled the bourbon. "Yeah," I replied, noting blood on the seat and on the bottom of the steering wheel. On the floorboard on the passenger's side was an almost empty bottle of bourbon, Jim Beam Black label.

With a hint of suspicion in his voice, he asked, "What are you looking for?"

"Just looking," I replied indifferently. "The family wanted me to take a look at it. Make some kind of arrangements."

"They going to be the ones paying storage on it?"

I looked at him through the windshield. Out of a perverted curiosity, I asked, "How much is the storage?" I opened the glove compartment. Like Newt had said, it was empty.

"Fifty a day."

Fifty a day! Highway robbery, but it was practiced by every salvage yard in the country. Tow a vehicle, charge outrageous storage, then, when the sum exceeded the value of the vehicle, file a mechanic's lien, and you had yourself a damaged vehicle from which you could sell the parts.

I nodded. "Sounds fair. I'll have to talk to the family, but what about if they just signed the truck title over to you?" I stepped back and closed the door. "The parts off an old truck like this might be demand around here, huh?"

A frown furrowed his brow, but I knew he was just stalling. With a shrug, I continued. "Otherwise, I can't guarantee what they'll do. They sure won't haul it back to Austin in the shape it's in, and you'd have to go to the time and expense of placing a lien on it. This way, there's no hassle for either party."

With feigned reluctance, he grunted. "Reckon that's as fair as a body could want."

Jack scooted around in the seat to face me when I climbed back in. "Any luck?"

"Yeah. As much as could be expected."

"Now what?"

"Now," I replied, heading back to Elysian Hills, "we'll pack Justin's belongings."

For the next few minutes, we drove in silence. Jack sucking on his Budweiser, and me reliving the last conversation I had had with Justin. I remembered how excited he was with his discoveries, discoveries just about everyone else claimed never existed.

What had Justin discovered? And were the items in his shack? Were they the reason for his death? Or was it really just an accident?

It was almost noon by the time we reached Elysian Hills. I started to pull in at Hooker's for lunch but on impulse headed on down the road to the other convenience store, Fuqua's.

Sam Fuqua was a short, swarthy man with a perennial grin on his face. His black hair was combed back, and his thin mustache was neatly trimmed.

Sam grinned. "Hey, I remember you." His grin faded. "You're the one who took Justin back to his family." He shook his head. "Me, I wish you had not took the boy back. He was a good boy. Now—" He shrugged. "I miss him."

"I know." I introduced Jack to the slight man and glanced around the store, which appeared to contain just a little bit of everything. Unlike Hooker's, there was no restaurant. "Got any sandwiches? My friend and me are getting hungry."

He pointed to the cooler. "Over there. Microwave next to it."

Jack nuked two barbeques while I opened a ham and cheese on wheat and popped a can of Diet Coke.

Sam indicated the worn chairs surrounding the space heater. He grunted. "Sit. Take a load off." I sat. He poured some coffee and came to join me. Jack waited at the microwave for his sandwiches. Sam frowned. "Terrible thing, the wreck. Justin was a good man." He paused, and his grin grew wider. "Some think he was kind of touched."

"You mean the UFO stuff?"

The slight man grew serious. "Me, I don't know nothing for sure. My grandparents, they come to America in 1903. We been here since. I'm just a dumb country hick, but some of the things Justin told me about . . ." He paused and raised his eyebrows. "I don't know if they be true or not. I'm not a smart man, but some of the stories he mentioned, they be too crazy not to maybe have a little truth in them."

I was so engrossed in his remarks that I forgot all about my ham and cheese. "Such as?"

Sam glanced around the store, then smoothed his thin mustache with a thumb and forefinger. "Justin, he show me a piece of metal." He shook his head. "He said he found it, but I think he was making a joke on me. I don't know how, but what he had, I never seen nothing like it before. I figure he got it from some joke shop when he was gone down to Austin."

Chapter Thirteen

Jack waddled up and plopped down in one of the worn chairs. He was too busy chowing down his two barbeques, bag of chips, and Dr. Pepper to pay attention to us.

I remembered the skin of the aircraft of which Justin had spoken. I leaned forward. "Was it a piece of metal that unfolded itself?"

Sam's eyes twinkled. "That's it. You see it too, huh? I figure he must be joking. But when I look at the metal, I can't see how it does that. I tell Justin it is some new invention that the Army made, but he just laughed and shook his head. He tell me that soon I would see what he meant. That the Army didn't have nothing to do with it."

At that moment, the door opened, and a blast of cold air swept in. Two weathered cowmen wrapped in wool mackinaws, their western hats tugged down over their ears, stomped in, slapping their hands vigorously on the arms of their heavy coats. "Whew! Hey, Sam, it's getting colder out there," one shouted as the other indicated the cigarettes behind the register.

While Sam Fuqua tended his customers, I stared hypnotically into the tiny blue flames of the space heater. Soberly, I realized the only explanation for what Sam had seen was the skin of the spacecraft.

Without warning, the enormity of the incident, the worldwide ramifications of the phenomenon, the absolute proof of all we believed impossible, if it were true, stunned me.

I was still staring at the fire when Sam returned. He pulled his chair closer to the fire. Outside, the wind howled around the corners of the building and under the eaves. I shivered.

He wagged a short finger at me. "I tell you what. You go see Marvin Lewis. He knows all about what goes on around here." He nodded emphatically. "Some laugh at him, but that one, he don't care. He say what he think."

I thanked him. "That's where we were headed next."

Jack frowned at me after we climbed into the pickup and I turned the heater to full blast. "What was that all about, Tony? Sounds mysterious."

With a chuckle, I replied. "How about it, Jack? You believe there are people on other planets?"

His brow knit. He snorted and shook his head. "You mean the little green man with the big head business? Hey, no way."

I laughed. From what I had heard, except for the color, that was the exact description of the pilot from the alleged spaceship. "I don't either, but Justin Chester did, and I have the strangest feeling that somehow, that spaceship business seems to be mixed up in his death."

He snorted. "Space aliens! Those are just stories made up by wackos who are always seeing flying saucers and such garbage." He tapped a finger against his chest. "No such thing, and you can take that straight from Mr. Cynic here."

I chuckled. "Mr. Cynic, huh?"

"You bet. Mr. Cynic when it comes to that alien junk."

During the short drive to Marvin Lewis' place behind the UFO museum, I couldn't help puzzling over Justin's facial injuries being as slight as they were. I'm not real swift, but logic suggested that I might be right about Justin's being dead for several hours before he went into the creek. If he'd been alive, his forehead would have slammed into the steering wheel, and there would have been copious bleeding.

The slight bruise Tricia mentioned had to be a result of rigor's preventing the full impact. I grimaced, still puzzled. The imprint, she said, was the size of a dime. What could he have struck to cause such an impression?

Regardless, I couldn't see any way he could have slammed the *back* of his head against the wheel. I glanced at Jack. He'd been with me on a few cases, and sometimes when I bounced theories off him, he actually provided some helpful feedback. I cleared my throat. "Suppose you were driving along in your Cadillac, just a lap belt. You run into a wall. What part of you hits the steering wheel?"

He grunted and patted his protruding belly. "What do you think? My stomach."

"Besides that," I replied, grinning.

He arched an eyebrow. "My face, naturally."

"What about the back of your head?"

He snorted and twisted left and right in his seat belt. "Ain't no way."

"That's what I figured."

"So? What's the big deal?"

"So, the big deal is that when Buck Ford—he's a local—found Justin, the dead man was still buckled in. There was no injury to his face, only to the back of his head. And a tiny mark on the forehead," I added.

Jack had been around me long enough to ask the next question. "What about the autopsy?"

Shaking my head, I replied, "There wasn't one. The justice of the peace here filled out the death certificate. He didn't see a need for an autopsy. When the family got the body, they had it cremated."

He leaned his shoulder against the door and stared at me. He pursed his lips. "So are you thinking what I think you're thinking?"

I chuckled. "I'm just a suspicious person, Jack. When I first started in this business, my boss told me to mistrust everyone. What he meant was, don't accept what you're told. Instead, find out for yourself."

Jack shrugged. "Makes sense." He stiffened. "Hey, look at that, would you?"

He was pointing to the UFO museum.

"That's where Justin Chester lived, in a room in the back. We're going to see the owner now."

A frown knit his brow. "I wasn't paying a whole lot of attention, but seems like I heard that old man back at the store mention something about UFOs."

I nodded to the redbrick house on the crest of the hill. "That's what we're going to find out."

Marvin Lewis was a wizened little man knocking on his ninety-first birthday. He had a full head of white hair, and his blue eyes twinkled as if they possessed a joke of their own.

When I introduced myself, the twinkle went out of his eyes. He studied me suspiciously. "Was it you out here prowling around last night?"

"What?" I stared at him, temporarily confused. "I'm sorry, Mr. Lewis, but I don't know what you're talking about. I've never been up here before except when I came with Justin Chester to pick up his belongings."

He studied me closely, then grinned. He threw open the door and invited us in. "Yeah. I remember you. I heard you was about. Justin, he told me about you. Come on in, come on in. It's cold out. Let's go back to the kitchen, where it's warm."

The house was old. It smelled musty. Its walls held the pictures and mementos of several generations. A body could have spent days studying the history tacked and pasted on the faded wallpaper.

As in all old homes, the kitchen was strictly utilitarian. All four burners in the stove blazed, and, mixed with the rich aroma of coffee, filled the room with satisfying warmth. A thick coat of smoke and grease stained the cabinets and walls. In the middle of the kitchen sat a chrome and yellow Formica dinette set.

He gestured to the table while he headed for the cabinet and the automatic coffeemaker. "How about some coffee? Take the chill off."

"Sounds good," I replied for the two of us. "You had some prowlers last night, you say?"

Speaking over his shoulder, he replied. "Yep. Around two

or three this morning. By the time I got out there, they was gone."

I explained why we were there. "The family wanted me to come up and gather Justin's belongings."

After filling three cups, Lewis opened a cabinet and pulled down a bottle of Jim Beam Black label bourbon and splashed a dollop into one cup. He held the bottle out to us. "I like to flavor my coffee."

Jack spoke up. "I like a lot of flavor."

Marvin laughed and "flavored" our coffee liberally.

As he served the steaming liquid, he said, "Terrible thing about Justin. I really liked that man."

"Yeah. Nice guy."

Marvin slid in at the table and blew on his coffee.

I continued. "As I understand, he was really caught up in this UFO business around here."

Jack, now curious about the UFOs, looked at the old man with anticipation.

Peering suspiciously at me from under his bushy white eyebrows, Marvin said. "He tell you about what he found?"

A tiny flame of anticipation coursed through my veins. At least he hadn't brushed the UFO business aside, as everyone else did. "He mentioned some things, but he never showed me anything."

The old man continued to study me. "When he came here a few months back, he only had a few dollars. There was something about him." He shook his head thoughtfully. "Like he was looking for something. I don't know, maybe a place to call home, maybe a place where he felt like he could belong. I guessed from talks we had later that he didn't have much of that when he was growing up."

I thought about the Chesters and their money and the palpable rancor that swirled about them like a Central Texas tornado. Marvin Lewis was a perceptive man.

"Anyway," he continued after sipping his coffee, "I had a room at the back of the museum. Kinda like a storm cellar. You got to go down a flight of stairs to get to it. Like I said, he only had a few dollars, and I wasn't using the room, so I told him to stow his gear there. Keep the museum clean, and he could stay there for nothing. A couple days later, he got a job at the school." He paused, raised his eyebrows, and said, "Not much more to say except he started asking a bunch of questions about the UFO that landed here in 1897."

Jack snorted. "You got to be kidding. There's no such thing as UFOs."

A tolerant grin slid over the old man's wrinkled face. "Well, son, some say yes, some say no. Most folks around here say it was a hoax. I ain't never read them, but I've been told that down at Hooker's store, there's a letter Jim Bob Houston wrote to a newspaper back in the fifties claiming that his grandpa and two other men made up the story, as well as an article in a Dallas paper about it."

I nodded. "They're there. I've read them."

Frowning, Jack asked, "You mean you never read the letter, even after all these years?"

The older man smiled. "Never did."

"Why?"

Marvin sneered. His next words sent chills up my spine. "I ain't never bothered to read it because I know for a fact it is a lie."

Jack's jaw hit the table.

Mine wasn't far behind.

Chapter Fourteen

Jack caught his breath. He looked up at me suspiciously, then cut his eyes at Marvin. "You're saying there was a UFO? Did you see it?"

The old man pushed back from the table and shuffled over to a window. "See that hill right out there? The one that's got a bunch of fresh holes in it?"

We both peered out the window over the sink.

The crest of the grassy knoll was pocked with filled-in holes.

"What about it?" Jack asked.

"My grandfather, S. D. Lewis, he was a judge. Well, he had a windmill out there. Pumped water for his cows. My pa was just a younker when it happened. One night when I was about ten or so, Grandpa Lewis and I was sitting out on the porch of the old home, and that's when he told me that one night in April about twenty-odd years before, a spaceship crashed into his windmill, tearing it down and destroying the ship. They found the pilot. He was dead. He was short and odd looking with a head the size of a watermelon."

Jack whistled softly.

The old man hesitated, his eyes looking back into the hazy memories of his life. He chuckled. "Grandpa Lewis was always telling stories, stretching them real far. I figured that was what he was doing then. My pa was on the porch with us, and I looked up at him. He had a funny grin on his face, half serious, half laughing. He just nodded and said, 'Pa's right, boy. This ain't one of his stretchers.'"

By now, Jack was absorbed in the tale. So much for Mr. Cynic, I told myself.

Personally, I tried to take the story with that proverbial grain of salt. I believe very strongly that if a person tells a lie long enough, he'll come to believe it. And there is no one more indignant than a liar who is discovered. The question was, which group in Elysian Hills was lying—those who believed, or those who scoffed?

His voice now registering only a minimal degree of skepticism, Jack whispered, "They saw the body?"

The old man continued staring out the window at the grassy knoll on which the windmill had once sat. "That's what they said." He turned back and fixed us with his steady blue eyes. "The pilot was short—three, four feet. Big head. According to Grandpa Lewis, a few neighbors come over to see what was going on. They had seen the spaceship fly over real low that morning and were close enough to hear the noise when it crashed. They all decided right then to bury the dead pilot in the cemetery but keep the grave hidden."

Jack drew a deep breath. "Why would they do that? They

probably could have made a bunch of money showing off the body."

Marvin Lewis smiled sadly at Jack. "And have people coming from all over, trampling your crops, upsetting your way of life?" He shook his head. "No, siree."

"Well, yeah, but—" Jack looked up at me for help.

I shrugged. "That was over a hundred years ago, Jack. People were different then."

"Yeah, but—"

"I've asked myself that same question, Mr. Edney," Marvin replied. "I still don't know."

"Well, has anybody ever dug him up?"

Shaking his head, Marvin replied, "They hid the grave. Everybody agreed that only a few would bury him. Them that knew the location carried it to their own graves." He paused and added, "But Justin worked hard trying to find the location."

With a heavy dose of skepticism coating my words, I replied, "He have any luck?"

Marvin shrugged. "If he did about the burial site, he didn't say anything to me about it. As far as the other stuff, that's why the hill out there is all dug up. Justin spent several days out there with a metal detector. He'd hear something, then he'd dig it up."

We returned to the table. I sipped my coffee, which was growing cold. Resting my elbows on the table, I leaned forward. "Did you see any of the stuff he found?"

"Some," Marvin replied with a tiny shrug. "I'd gone to visit my brother, Benjamin, over to Gainesville for three or four days when Justin—" He hesitated. "When the accident happened."

"Did he ever show you a piece of metal that unfolded it-self?"

He frowned and shook his head slowly. "No. Most of what I saw could have come from pieces of the windmill or any of a number of things. Grandpa Lewis rebuilt the wind-mill. There was a well house out there. They're all gone now, but as much as I hate to admit it, because he wanted it so much, those pieces Justin found could have been from broken pumps, sucker rods, wind generators, fan blades. Those parts could have been left over from any number of windmills over the last hundred years."

The old man must have spotted the frown on my face, for he added, "Oh, I believe it happened, but it's hard to imag-ine that anything would be left around after all that time."

Jack blew softly through his lips. "But it is possible, huh? Still, that is awfully hard to imagine."

I chuckled. "You've got plenty of company." I changed the subject. "If you don't mind, Mr. Lewis, we'll go out and pack Justin's things. Everything is just about wrapped up around here."

I wasn't really lying. I'd spoken with many who had known Justin; with those who had found him after the acci-dent; and those with whom he had shared his belief in UFOs.

Now, I knew Tricia Chester had suspected that her sib-lings had had something to do with the death of the younger brother, but I had found nothing to implicate them.

I had a couple of questions that puzzled me, such as the injury to the back of Justin's head, but then, all sorts of crazy things occur in accidents. As far as the aircraft skin, I'd have to see it to believe it.

The only person remaining with whom I wanted to visit was the justice of the peace. I'd do that tomorrow.

A few minutes later, I paused at the top of the steps leading down to Justin's room. "You coming down, Jack?"

He eyed the stairs leading into the ground. "No. Unless you need some help carrying stuff up."

I started down. "He didn't have that much."

The room smelled musty. I quickly packed Justin's clothing and the few personal items lying around. The rickety table he'd used for a desk was clean. I don't know why, but I had half expected sheaves of paper to be stacked upon it. On impulse, I removed the two-by-four in the doorjamb of his closet. I spotted a roll of papers bound by a rubber band.

Glancing over my shoulder toward the door, I hastily extracted the roll from the doorjamb. I remembered the sheet of aircraft skin Justin had mentioned, the same sheet of which Sam Fuqua had spoken. I peered back inside, but the cavity was empty. Puzzled, I rolled the papers out on the table and stared at the drawings.

There were no words on the first drawing, just a series of interconnecting lines. It appeared to be a schematic of Elysian Hills. One of the lines had an *S* curve in it, and I remembered Mabel Hooker's telling me that the Cemetery Road had an *S* curve. I adjusted the paper so the roads were oriented to their proper points on the compass.

The second held a grid of intersecting lines but nothing to indicate what they meant. At the juncture of two perpendicular lines near the top of the grid, Justin had drawn a tiny circle. From the circle, a diagonal line extended about half an inch.

The third page contained an inventory of what he had discovered: bolts, pieces of rusted metal, and one of the items was a five-by-four–inch piece of aircraft skin with hieroglyphics or symbols. At the bottom of the page, Justin had drawn several strange characters.

$$\text{ȣ ɤ ƕ ƞ}$$

My heart thudded against my chest. I shook my head in disbelief. Could these strange characters be the hieroglyphics Justin had told me about? They had to be.

Maybe I should hang around a while longer, I told myself.

The other papers contained notes he had garnered from the locals regarding the oral legends concerning the UFO that had crashed into Lewis' windmill. Even a cursory glance told me that the stories merely reprised the ones I had heard since I had been in Elysian Hills.

I heard footsteps coming down the stairs, so I quickly rolled the papers and slid them into the inside coat pocket of my tweed jacket.

Jack stuck his head into the doorway. "Need any help?"

Rising and looking around, I shook my head. "Nope. Finishing up. I don't know about you, but I'm ready to call it a day. Let's go pick up your car."

Up above, Marvin Lewis waved us down just before we left. He hurried out to my truck. "Get it all?"

"Wasn't much there, but I got it. By the way, any idea about what he did with the few pieces he dug up on the hill?"

Marvin frowned. "Nope. You might ask Harlan Barton. Sometimes he helped Justin with the digging and stuff to pick up a few bucks."

"Barton?" I frowned. "You mean that old man shuffling around town?"

"Yep. He lives out on Cemetery Road. Rundown shack just past the bridge. Can't miss the place. Of course, half the time he's drunker'n a skunk."

Thirty minutes later, we pulled into the parking lot of the Bucket Inn on I-35. My room had an extra double bed, so I had no compunction in suggesting Jack save his money. Bunk with me. I made arrangements at the desk. It was only a few bucks more, and I was on expenses.

On several occasions in the past, we've shared rooms. He wasn't a bad suite-mate, although at times when he'd had too much Budweiser, he snored like the proverbial chain saw. I usually rose early, and by the time Jack rolled out of bed, I was downstairs on my second cup of coffee. So we were never in each other's way.

I don't know about all the states, but I'd be willing to bet there is not a single truck stop in Texas that doesn't special-ize in chicken-fried steak, cream gravy, and French fries. And in gigantic portions.

Jack ordered the largest chicken-fried steak on the menu. I settled for the small one, and even then I left over half of it. While Jack was polishing off his repast and placing the remainder of my meal into a doggie bag for a midnight snack, I decided to take my pickup next door to the Valero station to fill up.

On impulse, I stopped off in the liquor store beside the motel and bought a bottle of Jim Beam Black label bour-bon. I might have some use for it the next day.

I shivered as I stood beside my pickup at the gas pumps.

The night had grown colder. My breath came in frosty puffs. After paying at the pump, on impulse I went inside and bought half a dozen scratch-off lottery tickets. I never won, but from time to time I took a fling. Who could tell? Maybe tonight I would become a millionaire.

While I was waiting for my change, I glanced out the window and spotted the familiar face of Lester Taggart. Bulldog Face himself.

By the time I got outside, he had disappeared around the corner of the motel.

Chapter Fifteen

I hurried after Taggart. When I reached the corner of the motel, I spotted a single vehicle leaving the parking lot. I couldn't make out the license number. All I could tell was that it was a small white car. Whether he was in that one or not, I had no idea.

At that moment, my cell rang. It was Danny. His connections at the funeral home assured him that the trauma was to the back of Justin's head. His face, except for a slight scuff that did not break the skin on his forehead, was unmarked.

Hanging up, I considered Danny's reply. Could my hunch be right? Someone had struck Justin on the back of the head and then driven the pickup into the creek? I reminded myself to visit George McDaniel the next day to see what light he could shed on Justin's injuries.

A blast of frigid air whistled down in front of the motel. I shivered. I could not see beyond the glow of the motel

116

lights, but from the endless Texas brags I'd heard, all that lay out there was an endless prairie, windswept and desolate, stretching all the way to the North Pole with nothing to break the wind but a couple of barbed-wire fences. What next?

Turning back to the motel, I made a mental note to call Tricia Chester first thing in the morning. I wanted to know what Lester Taggart was doing here.

It was the kind of morning to stay in a warm bed with the covers over your head. Outside, the wind howled, a mournful, chilling whine that drove the cold to the very marrow of your bones.

I rolled out of bed and called to Jack. "Hop up. We've got work to do this morning."

Downstairs, in a corner of the restaurant, I called Tricia and told her about Taggart.

"I have no idea why he was there, but I did ask Vanessa why she had him following me," Tricia Chester exclaimed.

I glanced at Jack across the breakfast table. He was completely absorbed in his blueberry pancakes and honey syrup. "And what did she say?"

"She said she was worried about me. My maid—" She paused and in an apologetic tone said, "You were right about her—the maid, I mean. She's the one who told Vanessa I was going out to the County Line that night."

"That's what I figured."

Then she continued. "Anyway, my maid told her I had been talking about using a detective agency to find Justin.

Vanessa said she was afraid I would hire an unreliable one. She even checked on your company with the Better Business Bureau and the local police."

For a moment, I was speechless. Either Vanessa Chester was a glib liar, or she hovered over her siblings like an old mother hen. And I didn't believe the latter. Although I had met the woman only twice, the second time at Justin's funeral, her demeanor did nothing to suggest a deep concern for anyone's welfare except her own.

I started to ask Tricia if she believed her sister, but she must have anticipated the question, for she continued. "I don't believe her, but that's what she said. And as soon as we hang up, I'm going to call her and find out what Taggart is doing up there!"

Taking a deep breath, I replied, "Well, he's here. Or was here." I paused, then, seeing that the conversation was at a dead end, added, "I should have everything tied up today or tomorrow."

"Why is it taking so long? Or have you discovered something?"

"Not really," I lied, then stretched the truth some more. "The folks around here thought a lot of your brother. These old country people, once they start talking, it's hard to get away from them."

I could see no reason to tell her of the unanswered questions in my mind. I didn't believe in any of the UFO nonsense, but there still existed a few items missing from the inventory list, the aircraft skin among them. If Sam Fuqua had not mentioned it, I never would have pursued it. The truth was, I was curious as to exactly what Justin had found. Whatever it was, there had to be a logical explanation for the properties it was said to possess—and why it was missing. In a way, I felt I owed it to the poor guy.

In the call Justin had made to me, he was obviously very excited. I could never forget his words. "I've got it, Tony. I told you I would, and now I have it."

And when I asked him what he had, he'd exclaimed, "Proof of the spaceship!"

He had also remarked that the sheet of metal had not set off his metal detector. He had discovered it while digging up other artifacts.

So now I was curious about what kind of discovery would lead him to make such a statement and what kind of metal on this earth would not set off a metal detector.

Before we left the motel, I purchased a throwaway camera from the gift shop downstairs.

Thirty minutes later, we passed the Elysian Hills Baptist Church on the left side of the narrow macadam highway. The sheriff's office was just beyond on the right.

I slowed as I approached Cemetery Road. On the left, Newt Gibons was climbing from his pickup. He was wearing the same baggy overalls he had worn the day before. I waved. He nodded.

He paused to watch as I turned onto the road behind his shop. I glanced into the side mirror and spotted him peering around the corner of his shop so he could see where I was heading.

A mile down the narrow road, I came upon a new section of barbed-wire fence on the left just beyond a shallow ditch. Tire tracks on the side of the ditch indicated where Justin had left the road. Fifty feet beyond was a large oak with a fresh scar in the rugged bark. I pulled to the side of the road and parked.

Jack frowned. "What's up? Why are we stopping?"

I reached for the camera. "This is where Justin Chester ran off the road. See that oak? That's the one he hit. I just want some pictures for the family." The truth was, the family could just as well do without the pictures. I wanted to take a look at the scene myself.

Justin's death wasn't as cut-and-dried as it seemed. There were too many unanswered questions. How could you explain the injury to the back of his head? What did the lines on the sheets of paper mean? Where was the piece of metal with hieroglyphics? And what was Lester Taggart doing at the motel the night before?

After snapping a shot of the repaired fence, I crawled through the barbed wire—a technique in itself—and snapped a couple of shots of the oak. The scar in the thick trunk was shallow, in keeping with the crumpled fender.

Several patches of shinnery—wrist-thick stunted oaks no more than head high—dotted the pasture. Beyond the tree was the gully.

I frowned. The gully was deep—thirty feet, at least. A narrow creek meandered along the bed of the ravine. The ground along the rim of the creek was scarred with tire tracks that obliterated the original ones. On the far bank grew a thicket of wild azaleas covered with blackberry vines.

I snapped a few more shots. On the way back to the pickup, I noticed a set of old tracks leading around and behind a patch of shinnery but dismissed them.

* * *

Jack raised an eyebrow. "Find anything?"

"Nope." I closed the door and sat staring out over the steering wheel. "I don't think so." I shook my head and looked back at the gully. "It's deep."

"How deep?"

I shrugged. "Twenty-five, thirty feet."

He groaned. "Must have been some impact when it hit."

"Yeah," I replied, shifting into gear and heading on down the road. I wanted to pay Harlan Barton a visit. I crossed my fingers he was sober.

After negotiating the *S* curve and rattling over the old bridge, I pulled up at a battered mailbox leaning to the left like a wobbly drunk. I hoped that was not a portent of Barton's condition. Rust pocked every inch of the box.

"What's here?" Jack asked.

"Old man by the name of Barton, I think. I hope," I replied, trying unsuccessfully to read the name on the mailbox. "Let's go up and see."

The farmhouse was a weathered gray two-story with a porch running the length of the house. One side of the house sagged, giving the porch the appearance of a matchstick snapped in the middle. Several panes of glass were broken from windows upstairs and down. Some had been covered with slats of wood, several of which had come loose and swung by one end from a single nail like a pendulum with each gust of wind.

Back in Louisiana, I'd seen houses like this out on the prairies, but they had all been deserted for years.

I stopped in front of the house.

Moments later, the front door opened, and a ragged figure peered out. A patchy gray beard grizzled his wrinkled cheeks. The ragged trousers he wore appeared three sizes too big. I stepped out and held up my hand. "Mr. Barton?"

He didn't answer, so I continued, identifying myself and explaining, "Justin Chester's family sent me up here to pick up his things. Marvin Lewis said you sometimes worked with Justin. I hoped I might be able to talk to you about him." I leaned back into the pickup and grabbed the bottle of Jim Beam. I held it up for him to see. "We didn't come empty-handed."

Five minutes later, we were seated around an ancient round oak table in the kitchen, a tiny pocket of warmth in the frigid house. To merely that say the room, the entire house, was cluttered could not begin to describe the extent of the chaos.

The only place I'd ever seen close to it was back in Central Texas in a battered mobile home in the middle of the Devil's Backbone hills. There I encountered an old codger who kept pet snakes in his house. He had a six-foot rat snake he had named Jefferson Davis that came out from under the couch every noon for a saucer of whiskey.

Glancing around the kitchen, I noted that Barton's cabinets and countertops were cluttered with dishes, pans, and farm items. When he had run out of room on the cabinets, he'd started around the walls. Stacks of magazines dating back to the thirties filled the halls, leaving only a narrow path to traverse from one room to the next.

I would not have been surprised one whit if old rat snake Jefferson Davis didn't have a couple dozen of his distant family members living among the junk.

Barton set three glasses on the table. I'll give him credit, he did wipe them out, but with the tail of his greasy flannel shirt. We both declined a drink, saying it was too early in the morning.

Barton filled the dingy water glass half full, gulped it down, and immediately replenished it. He licked his lips and leaned back in the worn chair, a satisfied grin on his craggy face. "Much obliged, boys. Now, what can I do for you?"

I explained that Justin's family had hired me to gather his belongings and talk to those who knew him. "They have no idea what he was doing up here, and they'd like to know. Last night, Marvin Lewis told us that sometimes you worked with Justin."

His rheumy eyes grew wary. "Sometimes."

I studied him for a moment, sensing that he knew more about Justin's business than I supposed. I pulled out the roll of papers from my inside pocket and spread them out on the table before him.

A single bulb hung directly over the table, illuminating it with a dim glow. "Have you ever seen these drawings?"

He studied them for a moment, then placed a wrinkled finger with a dirt-encrusted nail on one. "This here is Elysian Hills and Cemetery Road."

I showed him the sheet with the inventory of artifacts. "This is a list of what he claims he found, but I couldn't find any of the items, especially this one." I indicated the aircraft skin.

He took another long drink of whiskey and gave me a sly grin. "Wouldn't reckon you could. He gave them to me to hide."

"You?" I stared in disbelief.

I indicated the characters at the bottom of the page. "All of this, even the piece of metal with hieroglyphics on it?"

He pursed his lips. "I don't know about no high-er, what-ever you said, but that piece of metal has that kind of scratching on it." He pointed to the drawn characters at the bottom of the page. "I was there when Justin copied them from the metal. He didn't know what they meant either, but he said he was going to take them to someone at some college who studied things like that."

By now my heart was thudding in my chest like a twelve-pound hammer forging a horseshoe. I didn't know if I believed the old man or not, although he had given me no reason not to. "Was there something unusual about the metal? I mean, besides these characters?"

He looked from me to Jack and back again as if expect-ing us to laugh at him. "You, being city folk, might not think so, what with all these new inventions around today, but this metal, if you folded it in half and laid it down, it would straighten itself out."

Jack broke into a fit of coughing.

Barton continued, nodding to the sheet of paper with the grid penciled in. "That one," he said. "That's the cemetery. And see there, that circle on the juncture of those two grid lines?"

"Yeah. What about it?"

After taking another large swallow of whiskey, he replied. "From the middle of those two roads, exactly twenty feet southwest, is a metal rod in the ground. Justin put it there where I showed him. Buried it under the grass so no one would see it."

I frowned, not following the gist of what he was saying. "Why? Does it mark something?"

A sly grin curled his lips. "Reckon it does." He paused.

We waited impatiently. Finally Jack demanded, "So, what does it mark?"

The old man's grin grew wider. "That's where the space-man was supposed to be buried."

Chapter Sixteen

If Jack hadn't been coughing enough, Barton's declaration set him off again. I stared at the old man, searching for a smile in his eyes or on his thin lips. He looked up at me steadily and gestured to the three sheets of paper on the table. "Where did you find those?"

"Why?" I frowned.

"Because I couldn't. Justin was a good man. He told me if anything happened to him, to hide those papers, but I couldn't find them."

Confused, I shook my head. "If something happened to him? He said that?"

His weathered cheeks had taken on a light flush from the bourbon. His tone curt, he replied, "I don't lie none, sonny."

"No, no. I didn't mean that. It's just that I had no idea—well—"

"That there might be someone who didn't want the spaceman business stirred up?"

Jack leaned forward. "What do you mean by 'stirred up,' Mr. Barton?"

By now, the bourbon had loosened the old man's tongue. He eyed us slyly. "Could be someone don't want the grave dug up."

I studied him for several long moments, absorbing the implication of his words. I thought of the wound to the back of Justin's head. "Are you saying Justin's death was not an accident?"

He shrugged. "I ain't saying nothing except the man had a bad feeling. I don't know where or how he got it, but he told me if something happened to him, to hide them papers."

I remembered Marvin Lewis telling us about the prowler. "So that was you over at Lewis' night before last?"

"Yep. Got down into Justin's room, but I couldn't find them papers." He spotted Jack grinning at me. "Why you asking?"

"Lewis. He told us he had a prowler."

The old man cackled. "Marvin. He's got his own secrets. Him and Justin thought just alike about the spaceman, but neither of them knew the whole story. Not like I know it. And when I told Justin the spaceman wasn't there, he didn't believe me." He paused. "It was just after that Justin got his-self kilt dead."

It was my turn to be puzzled. "What story? About the spaceman?"

A sly gleam glittered in his eyes. "The spaceman. He didn't die."

I stammered. "But—"

Jack's eyes grew wide. "There's no such thing as space-men. That's impossible."

Barton downed another glass of bourbon. I eyed the bottle, thinking I might need a slug myself. Things were getting crazier and crazier.

"There's a heap of things we ain't never heard about, Mr. Edney. That don't mean they ain't there." Barton studied us. I had the feeling he was wondering if he should tell us the story or not. Finally, he continued. "I saw him once, when I was a younker—just a glimpse as he was leaving our barn before dark one night."

If Jack's eyes had grown any wider, they would have popped from his head and bounced around on the floor like marbles. And mine wouldn't have been far behind. "S-Saw who?" Jack gasped.

"Why, the spaceman." Barton continued. "I told my grandpa, and he told me the story about what took place. He was a young man when the ship crashed. He was one of them who was to bury the man, but on the way to the cemetery, they heard a noise. When they opened the box, the man was alive, so they turned him loose. Swore to each other never to say a word about it." He rose from the table and pointed out the rear window. "Back there is the Diablo Canyons. They're full of caves and tunnels. That's where he's said to be. I used to go out and see if I could find him, but I never saw him again. Never saw no sign of nothing except critters." He shrugged. "Can't tell, though. I might go out back tomorrow and catch a glimpse of him."

Jack asked the question I wanted to ask but couldn't build up the nerve to. To ask such a question meant I gave some credence to the bizarre story, and that was too much of a stretch for my own common sense. Jack muttered in disbelief. "You mean, you think he's still alive?"

He nodded matter-of-factly. "I don't know how Grandpa knew. Maybe he figured out how to talk to the man, but Grandpa told me he thought the spaceman could live two or three hundred of our years."

I didn't even bother to wipe out my glass. I splashed bourbon into it and gulped it down, not caring if the fiery liquid burned away the grease from the old man's shirt or not. But the story wasn't over yet.

Barton nodded to the grid on the sheet of paper. "There is something buried there. And I think maybe Justin figured out who it was." He paused. "I never told him. Maybe I should have, but I didn't know how far to trust him."

Jack scooted forward in his chair. "You mean in the spaceman's grave?"

I leaned forward. "Told him what? You know what's in the grave?"

"About twenty years or so ago, I was heading home from a friend's house early one morning. We'd had a night of drinking, so I was pretty snockered. I always cut across the cemetery. That night, I spotted a pickup parked about where I figured the spaceman's grave was. They was two men, and they was too far away to make out." He cackled. "Anyway, I was too drunk to recognize them even if I'd been closer. I passed out. When I woke up next morning, I didn't remember a thing. I started on home and stumbled over the fresh-dug ground. Then I remembered the pickup. For some reason, they'd dug up the spaceman's grave."

Jack's words were hushed. "No kidding?"

I arched a skeptical eyebrow. Memory gets hazy after twenty years, especially when fortified by whiskey.

Harlan Barton peered into the past, his rheumy eyes

clearing. "You see, when they went to bury the spaceman over eighty-odd years before, they didn't mark the grave, not with a marker. Instead, they buried the empty coffin fifty feet due south of an old white oak tree. Lightning destroyed the tree some years later, but at that time, there was enough stump left in the ground to take your bearings. That's how I know whoever was in that pickup put something down there. And they had to be kin of them what buried the spaceman's coffin in the first place."

I cleared my throat. "Why would they have to be kin?"

"Because," the old man snorted, "they knew the coffin was empty, a perfect hiding place for what they had in mind."

Jack looked around at me and whistled softly.

I rolled my eyes. This was fast turning into the kind of oft-told tale of which myths are born. "What do you figure they buried down there?" I studied him suspiciously.

His eyes grew wary. He ignored my question. "At first, I figured that in the next few days word would be out that the spaceman wasn't in the coffin, but I never heard no word about it." He paused. His rheumy eyes grew shrewd. "Now, you tell me, why wouldn't I hear nothing unless whoever dug it up didn't want nobody to know he'd done that?" And then, in a warning tone, he added, "On the surface, Elysian Hills looks like a simple little community, but there is a dark side that not many ever see."

His cryptic remark was too enigmatic for me to spend time analyzing. I figured I was listening to the ramblings of an old drunk. All I wanted were the items Justin had given him to hold. I touched my forefinger to one of the sheets of paper. "What about the items on this inventory? Do you have them here?"

A sly grin played over his weathered face. "I hid 'em good. Real good." He nodded to the kitchen window. "In one of the seed bins. Out in the barn."

Jack spoke up. "Let's go get them. I can't wait to see that piece of metal you were talking about."

For several long moments, Barton studied us, then nodded. He rose, staggered slightly, then grinned. "Let's go out the back way. When we come back in, I'll tell you what I found when I dug up the spaceman's grave." He was beginning to slur his words. "A bunch of folks is going to be mighty surprised."

I gaped at him in disbelief. "You dug it up?"

A sly grin played over his thin lips as he reached for the doorknob. "It was a full moon that next night. The dirt was fresh. The small casket was only a few under the ground. Didn't take long at all. I—" He opened the kitchen door and suddenly stiffened. He turned slowly to us, an expression of disbelief on his face. His bony hand clawed at his chest. He opened his lips to speak, but all that came out was a raspy gasp, and he collapsed.

A few minutes past three. Noble's Funeral Home loaded the gurney holding Harlan Barton into a long black hearse for the drive to Reuben. I stood on the porch with Justice of the Peace George McDaniel while the sheriff spoke with the driver of the hearse.

A lanky man in his early seventies, McDaniel grunted. "No disrespect intended, but if folks keep dying around here like they have the last few weeks, there ain't going to be no Elysian Hills." He chuckled and glanced at me.

"Has been busy," I replied. "I'd been meaning to visit with you about Justin Chester."

He shrugged. "Best ask the sheriff. I was down to Fort Worth when it happened. He took care of things." He grinned at my surprise. "We're just small-time folks here, Mr. Boudreaux. We got to work together when things happen. Know what I mean?"

"The death certificate said Justin was drinking."

McDaniel nodded. "When I saw the truck down at Newt's garage before he had it towed, it smelled to high heaven of whiskey."

I looked at him in amazement, well aware of the casual manner in which public affairs were handled in small towns. After all, I grew up in one, and more than once I saw officials acting in capacities beyond their own jurisdiction. It was a way of life in Louisiana. Same in Texas. Probably the same everywhere.

At that moment. Sheriff Perry headed back toward us as the hearse pulled onto the dirt road for the drive to Reuben. He glanced over his shoulder when he reached the porch and muttered, "When I go, I hope it's fast like that."

"Yeah," Jack muttered.

Sheriff Perry grunted. "Been expecting something like this for years."

McDaniel chuckled. "Yep. Old Harlan, he was probably the primary reason Jim Beam stayed in business so long. Alcohol ate his brain away."

Sheriff Perry laughed, but I just stared after the hearse.

Jack spoke up. "He have any family?"

"Nope," McDaniel replied. "Last of the clan." He gave his head a shake. "The Bartons were one of the first families to settle here back in the 1850s." His brow knit in sadness. "Seems like an awful shame. The Bartons in Elysian Hills is now nothing but history." He drew a deep breath and blew it out through his lips as he stepped down off the porch. "Reckon I best get back to the feed store, Sheriff. Getting close to the rush hour. Can't afford to miss no business."

"Yeah. See you later, George." Perry cleared his throat and turned to me. A little too enthusiastically, he said, "You're just about finished up around here, huh?"

I had the feeling Perry wanted us out of Elysian Hills. But why? Inadvertently, I glanced over my shoulder in the direction of the barn. I knew we weren't leaving until we had a chance to search for the list of items on the inventory. "Just about. I wanted to pay a visit to the cemetery. Take a couple pictures."

Perry frowned. "Pictures?"

I grinned at him. "Justin's family wants them. I suppose they want some memories of where he lived." With a shrug, I added, "Everyone to his own thing, right?"

Perry arched an eyebrow. "I suppose."

Perry stood on the porch watching us as we headed on down the road to the cemetery.

Jack scooted around in the seat. "What about the barn?"

"We'll go back when the sheriff leaves."

Several acres in size, the cemetery covered the crest of a gentle hill. We took one of the narrow lanes to the top and stopped. Ancient hickory and oak dotted the cemetery, splashing shadows onto the grassy carpet spreading over the hill.

Peering through the windshield at the rolling countryside, I was struck by a sense of peace and tranquility. "Pretty place, huh?"

Jack rolled his eyes. "Just a cemetery. Like all of them. Nothing but dead people."

I laughed. "You always could cut through the nonsense, you know that, Jack?"

"Well, once you seen one, you've seen 'em all." He glanced over his shoulder.

"I've always admired your capacity for compassion, Jack."

He ignored my sarcasm. "He's leaving."

"Huh?"

"The sheriff. He just turned onto the road back to town."

I looked into the side mirror as Sheriff Perry crossed the old wooden bridge. About a quarter mile ahead of him, a white car disappeared around the first curve in the *S*.

Taggert?

After the sheriff vanished around the same curve, I started the pickup and drove to the northeast corner of the cemetery.

"Where to now?"

"Let's see if we can find that metal rod Harlan Barton told us about."

With an indifferent expression on his face, Jack nodded. Suddenly, the lack of interest on his face crumpled into a grimace of alarm as my words soaked in. "The metal rod? Why?"

I shrugged. "Curious. Wondering it it's still there, and what it was Harlan found when he dug up the coffin twenty years ago."

Jack remained silent.

When we reached the marked spot on the map, I stopped the Silverado and climbed out. "From the middle of the junction, twenty feet southwest. Isn't that what he said?"

Jack remained in the pickup. "Yeah. I think so. Yeah, yeah. That's what he said."

I glanced back. "You coming?"

Glancing around the peaceful cemetery, he shook his head emphatically. "No. I'll wait here for you."

"Come on, Jack." I laughed. "After all, you said it yourself. There's nothing here but dead people." I paused and added. "And maybe one or two zombies."

He muttered a disgusted curse and climbed out.

I stepped off about twenty feet, then began feeling for the metal rod with the soles of my feet. "Here it is!" I exclaimed after several minutes of prodding the grassy carpet.

With obvious uninterest, Jack muttered, "So now you found it. What next?"

"Well," I replied, looking up and admiring the beauty and tranquility of the peaceful scenery, "after we finish searching through the barn, we'll get us some shovels and dig up the casket."

Jack's eyes bugged out. "We'll what?"

Chapter Seventeen

We pulled around Barton's old house so the pickup couldn't be spotted from the road. The ancient barn was even closer to falling down than the house. About fifty feet long, the barn was typical of such construction in the late nineteenth and early twentieth centuries. The two-story building was gabled at either end, and long sheds stretched the length of the barn on either side. On one side, the shed had collapsed. The other remained upright, sheltering rusting farm implements. The double-wide opening to the barn was canted several degrees to the right. One door had fallen, and the other hung by a single hinge.

Jack whistled softly. "You're not going to go in there, are you? Finding that stuff the old man talked about would be like searching for a needle in a haystack, Tony. Impossible. Besides, a strong wind might come up and blow the whole shebang down on you."

I had the same sense of trepidation. On the other hand,

Barton said he had hidden the items on the inventory list inside the barn, in a seed bin. I wanted to see the items, especially the piece of aircraft skin. "Look, he hid them in the seed bin. There couldn't be more than one or two seed bins in the barn."

Jack remained skeptical. "What's a seed bin?"

Taking a deep breath, I studied the rickety barn. "It could be where he kept the feed or maybe where he stored grain. I'll just have to look."

With a dubious grunt, he replied, "Okay. Just be careful."

"Don't worry. You wait outside." I grinned at him. "Tell you what. If it looks like the thing is starting to fall, throw your shoulder into it and give me a shout. Okay?"

He snorted. "Funny, funny."

The corral fences were down, so we just stepped over them and waded through the weeds to the gaping door. A broken hoe handle lay on the ground. I picked it up and banged one end against the ground to shed its dirt and mud. I figured the barn was probably home to every imaginable bird, bat, spider, and reptile indigenous to this part of the state, although, cold as it was, I didn't figure I had to worry about the latter two.

I eased through the door and into the shadows of the barn. I jumped when the sudden flutter of wings sounded. Tiny objects, frightened by my sudden appearance, darted through the air. A shadowy figure dashed across the ground through the stripes of sunlight shafting through a hole in the roof. In spots, weeds grew rampant. The collapsed shed was covered with vines.

Pausing inside so my eyes could adjust to the darkness, I peered around the barn, searching for a seed bin. For a few moments, my mind wandered, thinking of all this old barn had seen over the last hundred years, of all that had taken place within its walls: the laughter, the cursing, the joking—the living. And now it was gone, forever. Just a hollow, empty shell of what it had been, like Harlan.

I jerked myself back to the present. In the still-upright shed were parked several farm implements, frozen with rust. I recognized a cultivator, disks, chisel plows, and seed drills. Behind them sat a rusted tractor with metal wheels. I had no idea how old it was, only that it had been ancient well before my time.

Near the rear of the barn, I found a door held closed by a small hook latch and a drop bar. When I pulled it open, a dark object shot out and with a frightened squeak disappeared into the shadows of the barn.

I peered inside. There was enough light to see that the room had been used to store feed and seed. Empty sacks, covered with rat droppings, lay about the floor. Using the hoe handle, I moved the bags around but found nothing except more rat droppings, cockroaches, and, despite the cold, even a couple of spiders. I studied the walls, looking for crevices into which Barton might have stuffed the items, but discovered nothing.

On impulse, but with great care, I climbed the ladder to the lofts and searched through them.

I found nothing.

After another few minutes, I gave up the search.

We headed back to Reuben. I didn't want to purchase shovels from McDaniel at the feed store for fear word would get back to Sheriff Perry.

Digging up graves anywhere without permission is illegal,

and though I have at times on other cases stretched, bent, and twisted the law, I've tried not to blatantly break it. Not like I was planning to that night.

When we crossed the wooden bridge after leaving the cemetery, I glanced in the direction of Justin's accident, but the growth of brush and vines on the east bank shielded the spot from view. A bell rang in the back of my mind, but for the life of me, I had no idea why.

On impulse, I stopped and took a couple of snapshots from the bridge in the direction of the accident, hoping that later, when I viewed the pictures, I would remember whatever it was that was evading me at the moment.

A few miles beyond Elysian Hills, Jack grunted. "Wish I thought to bring along a beer. Why don't you pull in at the first place we see, and I'll pick up a case?"

It was times like this that I questioned my commitment to AA. I wanted a beer, and I was going to have one. Maybe I should stop fooling myself and quit AA. At least I wouldn't be making excuses all the time.

Jack continued. "What do you think Barton found in the grave, Tony?"

All I could do was shake my head. "No telling."

"Barton seemed to think that maybe Chester's death was not an accident. What do you think?"

I pondered his question. I wasn't really sure what I thought. "Hard to say. Back in Austin, I learned there was this guy looking for Justin the same time I was, but he had an ironclad alibi for the day of Justin's accident." I paused, then decided to keep rambling. Believe it or not, sometimes I even come up with some worthwhile ideas when I'm just talking about whatever comes to mind.

"When I first came here, I was looking for a missing man. That was all. I found him, took him back to his family, and the next thing I know, he's dead. Killed in an accident that I still can't—" I froze, a vivid image flashing in my mind of the view of the accident scene from the bridge. Suddenly I realized what had set off the clanging of bells in my head.

Slamming on the brakes, I ran onto the shoulder, made a U-turn, and headed back to Elysian Hills.

Jack hung on for dear life. "Hey! What the—"

I ignored him, remembering Buck Ford's explaining how he'd spotted the truck. *It was getting dark when I hit the bridge. If I hadn't been looking, I wouldn't have seen it. The truck was brown.*

"Tony! What's wrong? Where are we going?"

Flexing my fingers on the steering wheel, I muttered, "I think we've just stumbled neck deep into a swamp full of alligators, Jack."

I drove across the wooden bridge, turned around, and stopped at the end of it. I squinted into the growing dusk at the accident scene. "You tell me, Jack. Could you see a pickup in the creek from here?"

He grunted. "Which way do I look?"

I pointed to the oak in view above the brush lining the bank. "There."

"I can't see a thing," he replied. "That underbrush blocks my view of the creek." He looked around at me. "So what?"

I studied him a moment. "So, the man who found Justin's truck said he saw it from right about here."

Jack raised an eyebrow as if to say "no way." "He must have X-ray vision or something, then."

Shifting into gear, I headed back to the motel. I had a lot of work ahead of me.

In Reuben, while I picked up a couple of shovels and a pick, Jack popped into a sporting goods store and bought himself a warm parka.

Back at the motel, I pulled out my notes.

"Aren't you hungry? I'm starving," Jack said.

Without looking at him, I replied, "Bring me a hamburger and fries."

"That's all?"

A burger and fries was nothing more than an appetizer for Jack. "That'll do it, thanks."

After he left, I pulled out my stack of index cards. Each evening, I transfer information on the cards to my laptop. A couple of years back, I stumbled onto the USB portable drive and, pardon the metaphor, fell in love with it. I carry a second portable drive on which I back up the first after every use.

Needless to say, counting my note cards, my hard drive, and the two portables, I seldom lose any work if my laptop takes a crash dive.

But I do my primary work from the note cards. Now, if my IQ was up there at the genius level, perhaps I could keep everything in my head. But it isn't, and I have to find ways to cope with a bad memory. The note cards are the solution. With one incident per card, I can shift them around, allowing me the opportunity to look at events from different perspectives.

So, after Jack left, I started back at the beginning. My first stop in Elysian Hills was at the sheriff's office, when Sheriff

Perry failed to recognize the picture of Justin Chester or his name, although he had recently run a criminal check at the request of the elementary school principal, Georgiana Irwin.

My second visit began at the same place—the sheriff's office—where I learned that Buck Ford was the one who found the truck.

Suddenly I paused and thumbed back through the sheriff's cards. According to him, he'd been out at his place a couple of hours when he heard about the accident.

I looked back at the cards I'd made when I spoke with Mabel Hooker. According to her, just after she closed up, Buck Ford banged on her door to use the telephone. She said she was surprised Ford had managed to contact the sheriff at home, for Perry had passed her store only minutes earlier and might not have had time to reach his place.

And yet he had told me he had been home a couple of hours, treating sick cattle. Why the discrepancy in time?

I continued reading through my note cards. I paused and nodded with satisfaction when I came across the one that quoted Buck Ford as saying that if he hadn't been looking, he wouldn't have seen the pickup because it was brown.

Impossible! Underbrush blocked the scene from anyone on the bridge.

I leaned back and studied the cards. It doesn't take a genius to spot a goat in a flock of sheep, and it didn't take a genius to see that something was out of kilter in Elysian Hills.

Chapter Eighteen

By the time Jack returned, I was exhausted. Like my Grandpère Moise always said, I had stumbled across more loose ends than you'd find in a worm farm.

Jack handed me the bag with my burger and fries. "We still going to the cemetery tonight?"

"Yeah." I pointed a crisp French fry at a map on my desk. "But we're not going through Elysian Hills. I don't want to stir up any attention. Cemetery Road connects with a small town by the name of Rayford a few miles south. We'll come up that way."

We pulled onto the interstate around midnight. I kept my eye on the rearview mirror. Most of the headlights moved on past us, but I noticed that one set exited with us at Rayford.

I grinned in relief as they continued past the corner at which we turned, but a few minutes later, as we headed north toward Elysian Hills, a pair of headlights fell in about half a mile behind and followed us for a few miles before turning off.

Thirty minutes later, we eased to a halt in the cemetery. There was enough of a moon not only to see what we were doing but also to cast fathomless shadows that caused the hair on the back of my neck to bristle. In the distance, an owl hooted. A second answered.

Jack jumped. "What was that?"

"Just an owl, that's all."

At that moment, a coyote yipped several times and ended with a plaintive howl.

"That wasn't an owl!" Jack exclaimed.

"No, it wasn't. It was a ghost. Now start digging."

Jack jerked around. "What?"

"Just dig!"

A few minutes later, about four feet down, we hit the three-foot long casket, which, to my surprise, was still intact. I tied a handkerchief over my nose. Jack followed my example. Using the pick, I pried the lid off the wooden casket.

I've seen enough disinterred remains not to be surprised by what is revealed when a casket is opened. I've seen fifty-year-old remains that look as if they could get up and walk. Others, less than ten years old, were only pale bones.

But this time, when I threw the lid back and Jack flicked on the flashlight, I did a double take.

Jack whistled in amazement.

We stared at the interior of the coffin for several seconds. "That sure isn't no midget's bones," Jack muttered, staring at the skeletal remains that had been cut in half to fit into the small casket.

"Turn off the light," I said hastily. I pulled the throwaway camera from my pocket and snapped several shots. "All right. Let's cover this up and get back to the motel."

"Who do you suppose it was?" Jack whispered as we hurriedly shoveled the soil back into the grave.

"No idea, but that's who Harlan Barton saw being buried that night he told us about."

"Why didn't he report it to the sheriff?"

I padded the last of the soil down. "That's a good question, Jack. A real good question. I'm awful curious about the answer myself."

At that moment, a pair of headlights came over the hill from Rayford. Holding my breath, I watched as the small vehicle passed the cemetery, bounced over the bridge, and disappeared around the S-curve. I couldn't identify the make, but there was enough moonlight to see that it was a small white vehicle.

"A couple of kids looking for a lovers' lane, huh?" Jack chuckled.

I didn't laugh. Lester Taggart was foremost on my mind.

Before we reached Rayford, we tossed the shovel and pick out of the pickup. At a carwash off I-35, we washed down my Silverado, making sure no soil remained on the tires or body. Then we cleaned out the interior. Unless I was mistaken, someone might be paying us a visit in a few hours, and I was very curious about who that someone might be.

I was mistaken. No one came to see us, so midmorning Jack and I headed back to Elysian Hills. I wanted to talk to Marvin Lewis and Mabel Hooker. I wasn't really sure just what I was trying to do, but the more I considered the

circumstances of Justin's death, the more convinced I was
that he had been murdered.

But why? What was the motive behind his death? It
couldn't have been merely because of the UFO business.
There was no evidence of the spaceman's grave's being recently disinterred, but could Justin have put together a sound
enough theory of the contents of the grave that drove someone to kill him before he could expose them?

I pondered the theory, then pushed it aside for one that
made more sense, one that was supported by the grid he had
drawn. He was killed simply because he had discovered the
location of the grave. And whoever had placed the grisly
contents into the grave twenty years earlier had to stop Justin
Chester from digging them up.

One thing was certain: the remains in the grave did not belong to a three-foot spaceman, which, like it or not, supported
Harlan Barton's assertion that the community had not buried
the dead pilot. I refused to give any credence to the remainder of his assertion that they had turned the spaceman
loose—or that one had ever existed, for that matter.

As far as I was concerned, the burial of an empty coffin
was part of the hoax being perpetrated by the townsfolk. The
only fact I clung to was that the remains down in the casket
were those of a human, a human of this earth.

That was the most sensible idea I could come up with. But
who was the killer? The only two people involved in Justin's
death about whom I had questions were Sheriff Gus Perry
and Buck Ford.

Perry had claimed he didn't recognize Justin's name. Yet
he had recently run a criminal check on the man. In a small
hamlet like Elysian Hills, criminal checks had to be the

subject of gossip for at least a month. And how could the sheriff have not seen Justin riding his bicycle on his daily commute to and from the school? He rode past the sheriff's office twice a day.

And then there was Buck Ford, who had lied about spotting the pickup. Even if he had been elsewhere on the road, the gully was too deep to see it from anywhere other than the bank.

I figured that maybe the only way I could find my answers was to pick the memories of the old-timers in Elysian Hills— gently, of course.

Mabel Hooker was first, then Newt Gibons, then Marvin Lewis.

The morning had dawned cold, and as the day passed, the weather grew colder. Heavy, gray-ribbed clouds scudded overhead, promising rain or snow.

Wearing a Dallas Cowboys' Windbreaker over her gray sweat suit, Mabel Hooker grinned at us as we rushed in. "Morning, boys. Getting cold out there. Makes a body feel alive."

I shivered and rubbed my hands together briskly. "You can have it. All I want to do is stay curled up under half a dozen blankets on mornings like this. Give me warm weather and sandy beaches anytime."

"I don't know about you, Tony, but I could do with some coffee," Jack said, heading to the counter where the pot sat simmering. "Want some?"

"Yeah. Black." While he was pouring coffee, I nodded toward Cemetery Road. "Sad thing about Harlan Barton. Any word on when the funeral will be?"

She shook her head. "Nope. Sheriff said you was with him when he had the heart attack."

"He was fixing to take us out to his old barn. It hit him as soon as he opened the back door."

A grimace wrinkled her weathered forehead. "Poor old soul. He never hurt nobody. I always felt sorry for him. Didn't have nothing or no one. I'd invite him for Thanksgiving and Christmas. Sometimes he'd come, but most of the time he didn't. I'd usually end up taking him a covered plate." She paused. "That old barn of his must be falling down. What was he taking you out there for?"

I shrugged. "He was one of those UFO people like Justin. I guess that's why they hit it off. He wanted to show us something, but he died before he had the chance."

At that moment, Jack returned with our coffee.

"Show you something?" She snorted. "Now, what would that old rascal have out in that falling-down barn to show you?"

Jack started to reply, but I cut him off with a lie. "No idea."

Jack and I had taught together at Madison High School in Austin. I taught English, he coached, but just because he was a coach didn't mean he was dumb. He knew I had lied, but he also knew I had a reason. He grunted. "Yeah. We never got a chance to see what he wanted to show us."

I changed the subject. "When I was talking to Mr. Barton, he said something puzzling." I thumbed through my note cards until I found the one for which I was searching. He said, 'On the surface, Elysian Hills looks like a simple little community, but there is a dark side that not many ever see.'" I frowned at her. "What do you think he meant by that?"

She studied me for several moments, her ruddy face contorted in concentration, her unpainted lips pursed. "I don't know what he could have been talking about. The only thing exciting around here lately was Justin Chester. Before that, I suppose the only scandal was when Jim Bob's wife run off." She paused, her eyes narrowing slightly. Lowering her voice, she added, "There was talk she'd been fooling around with one of the local men. Nobody ever found out if it was true or not. Or if they did, they never said nothing."

I sipped my coffee. "When was that? Remember?"

Her eyes clouded in concentration. "Let's see. Eighty-three or so. I remember because that was the last year Elysian Hills had all twelve school grades in one building. I used to have a lot of after-school business, but when the seventh through twelfth grades moved to Reuben, I lost it all." Her eyes began to clear as her memory came rushing back. "It was in the spring, because we were all getting ready for the Easter parade down on the highway that we held every year. Sara Ann was her name." She laughed. "Lord, that was juicy gossip back then."

"So it was around that time that Jim Bob sold out, huh?"

"No, a couple years later, and then he left town." She hesitated, frowning. "There was some kind of confusion with the land, but," she added with shrug, "I don't remember what. They got it all straightened out, because after Marv bought Jim Bob's land, he sold Gus and Buck a couple sections each. That surprised a lot of us."

"Surprised? How's that?"

She laughed and gestured out the window. "You know how small towns are. "Folks get their feelings hurt. Buck and Marv never cared for each other. Family problems from way back. Hard feelings ever since, but they don't let it influence business."

I nodded to the oil wells dotting the rolling countryside. "I suppose they got the mineral rights with the land, huh?"

She shrugged. "Probably. Marv's got all he needs, but I can't say for sure."

As we drove down the highway to the automotive shop, Jack surveyed the wide-open country surrounding us. "I don't know how anyone can live out here, Tony. It's the most forsaken and desolate country I've ever seen."

Laughing, I replied, "You're just used to all the pine and cedar back in our neck of the woods, that's all. It's pretty much like this in parts of Louisiana except we have a few more swamps and alligators."

Newt Gibons had closed the large bay doors against the north wind. On either side of the shop, portable heaters blasted warm air into the cavernous room. The wind rattled the doors.

When Newt heard the door open, he pushed himself out from under a truck on a wooden crawler. The wheels clattered on the concrete floor. He sat up, wiping the grease from his hands. He was just as curt as he had been the first day. "What can I do for you?"

I hooked a thumb over my shoulder. "I just came from Hooker's. Mabel said you might be able to help me." The last was a lie.

He eyed Jack skeptically, then shrugged as he climbed to his feet. "If I can."

"When I was talking to Harlan Barton yesterday, he said

something puzzling." I pulled out the card and read it. 'On the surface, Elysian Hills looks like a simple little community, but there is a dark side that not many ever see.' " I looked up at him. "Any idea what he meant by that?"

Gibons studied me for several moments. Finally he replied in a drawl, "Harlan had hisself quite an imagination. Me, I don't think much about what goes on except in my shop and out at my place. Them that try to play their little tricks are welcome, as long as they don't play them on me."

Jack frowned up at me. I shrugged. Newt Gibons was just about as enigmatic as Harlan Barton had been. "What kinda tricks?"

He pursed his lips and shrugged. "Probably the same kind as they play back in the city where you come from."

Figuring I would get nowhere with this line of questioning, I changed the subject. "Mabel mentioned that Sara Ann Houston left her husband."

A twinkle came to his eyes. "She didn't lie about that."

"And then she said Jim Bob up and left town a few years later."

The twinkle in his eyes grew hard. "Well, sir, I suppose there's leaving town, and then there's leaving town."

Jack furrowed his brow. "What do you mean by that?"

"Just what I said. Some folk leave town one way, and some the other."

Jack and I exchanged looks, each knowing the other was thinking about the bones in the grave from the night before.

Chapter Nineteen

I studied the slight man for several moments while trying to frame my question. "Did Harlan Barton ever say anything to you about the spaceman's grave at the cemetery?"

A sly smile played over his lips. "Old Harlan told everybody about the spaceman."

"Do you think the spaceman is buried there?"

He chuckled. "I don't think there ever was one. Big joke. Letter over to Hooker's says so."

"Did the town ever hear from Sara Ann Houston after she left?"

"Not as far as I know."

"What about Jim Bob? He left town later. Mabel said there was some confusion over the land. Happen to know what she meant?"

"Nope."

"Did you know Jim Bob well?"

Finally he smiled. "He was a good man. Paid his bills on time. When he was mayor, he helped me get started here. I drove him to the hospital when he busted his leg." He touched his fingers to his left thigh. "Right here. Sawbones at the hospital didn't set it right. It was crooked."

"Ever hear from him after he left town?"

The smile faded. "No, and that wasn't like old Jim Bob. That's what I meant earlier. The way he left wasn't like him. No good-byes, no nothing. Here one day and gone the next. Not a word to his friends. Never could figure out how an old country boy could just up and leave all of this behind. Just look at this country. Have you ever seen anything as pretty and peaceful?" I couldn't see Jack, but I knew he was rolling his eyes at Newt's assessment of Elysian Hills.

"You think something might have happened to him?"

He eyed me suspiciously. "Did something?"

I gave him a crooked grin. "I've no idea. I'm just asking."

"Well, Mr. Boudreaux," he drawled, "you'll have to ask a smarter man than me."

Back in the pickup, I jotted my notes on cards. Jack watched. I knew him well enough to know what he was thinking. Finally he said, "This Houston guy left town back in eighty-five or six, and old man Barton claimed it was about twenty some-odd years ago he saw someone burying those bones out there." He paused.

Half smiling, I looked at him. "So?"

He snorted. "So, you know as well as me, those bones might be this Houston guy's."

"That's why," I replied, laying a hand on the throwaway

camera, "we're taking off early today and running down to a one-hour developing service in Fort Worth. I want to take a look at the bones in the casket."

"So you think the guy in the casket is Houston?"

"I don't know. It fits in with Gibons' remark that Houston had lived here all his life, so why up and move? And so suddenly. If they are Houston's bones, then Barton's remark about Elysian Hills 'having a dark side that not many ever see' would make sense."

He nodded. "And whoever the old man saw in the cemetery were the ones that killed the guy."

"Yeah."

"Any ideas?"

"No, but some questions. First, the sheriff claimed not to know Justin Chester when I first hit town, yet he'd run a criminal check on the man. The guy rode back and forth in front of the sheriff's office every day for months. In a place like Elysian Hills, you're telling me that a guy riding a bicycle up and down the highway wouldn't get your attention?"

"It would mine," Jack replied.

I continued. "Then there's Buck Ford. He said—"

Jack interrupted. "He's the one who said he saw the pickup from the bridge."

"Yeah." I flexed my fingers on the steering wheel. "He's the one."

Jack snorted. "He couldn't have."

"That's what I think."

On impulse I pulled into Fuqua's Stop and Shop. The temperature was dropping. A few drops of mist gathered on the windshield. We could be in for some unpleasant weather.

Sam Fuqua stroked his neatly trimmed mustache and greeted us with his perennial smile. We each bought a cup of coffee and gathered around the space heater. The diminutive man had no customers, so he joined us.

I sipped my coffee, enjoying the warmth of the steaming liquid filling me. "You've been in business here a long time, haven't you, Sam?"

"All my life. Me, I'll be seventy-three next month." He nodded emphatically. "My mama and papa, they opened this store." He made a sweeping gesture with one arm. "This is all I know."

"So, you've seen Elysian Hills grow."

He laughed and held his hands out to his sides. "She don't grow much no more. Not since the post office, it go to Reuben. That was before my time."

"Did you know Jim Bob Houston and his wife, Sara Ann?"

"Oh, yes. They come regular. Jim Bob and me, we grow up together." He gestured out back of the store to the creek that ran past the cemetery. "We spent a lot of summer days at the old swimming hole in the creek out there."

"Were you surprised when he left town?"

He nodded. "Me, I didn't expect that. This town is where his mama and papa is buried." With a sad knit to his brow, he added, "Of course, today, most of our young people, they go to Dallas or Fort Worth. Another hundred years, they won't be nothing left of Elysian Hills.

"What about his wife, Sara Ann? They said she had an affair with some local man, and that's what caused the breakup."

"I hear that." He tapped a fist against his heart. "That kill me, right here. She was good lady. I don't believe what they say about her."

I asked him about Harlan Barton.

He studied us warily, then replied, "He tell me many things, some hard to believe."

"About the spaceman? What did he tell you about that?"

His eyes shifted suspiciously from me to Jack. He lowered his voice. "He said the man was alive. I don't believe him. Once when I was driving Harlan home, I stopped at the side of his house. I saw something go in the barn. Like a child. When I tell Harlan, he just look at me and tell me to forget it. Not to never tell no one, or bad things would happen to the thing."

Jack muttered in disbelief, "You saw it, for sure?"

The small man smiled sadly. "I don't know what I saw, but it was small." Raising his eyebrows, he shrugged and held his hands, palms up, out to his sides. "Who knows? Maybe just shadows. I never see it again, and I been out to his place many, many times. And I never see it again."

"I heard that before Houston left, Marvin Lewis bought his place."

"Yes." His brow furrowed. "I don't know much, but once Marvin, he give Jim Bob money, and Jim Bob used his land as collateral. Then later, when Jim Bob, he want to sell, Marvin buys him out." He paused, then shrugged. "Me, I don't know no details." He paused and added, "You'd have to ask Marvin Lewis."

By now, the coffee was lukewarm. "Marvin Lewis, huh?" I remembered Mabel's saying that after Lewis bought the Houston place, he sold land to Sheriff Gus Perry and Buck

Ford. The PI in my blood made me want to learn more about the relationship among the three.

As we made a U-turn and headed back to Marvin Lewis' place, I noticed a white Honda pulling away from the feed store and heading northwest, away from us. I remembered the white vehicle that had driven past the cemetery the day before. Taggart? Or one of the locals?

Chapter Twenty

During the short drive to Marvin Lewis' place, Jack cleared his throat. "Do you think Fuqua really saw the spaceman, Tony?"

I considered the question for a moment. "Giving the old man his due, he saw something. I figure a shadow or a cat or something. Raccoon maybe, but not a spaceman."

There was a tone of earnestness in his voice when Jack replied. "You really don't believe in them, huh?"

I looked at him. "You're not starting to believe in the spaceman stuff, are you?"

Defensively, he shot back, "Hey, there's a lot of things we don't know." He paused, then, in an effort to save face, added, "I'm not saying I do, and I'm not saying I don't."

I laughed. "That's what I've always liked about you, Jack. When you take a stand, you take a stand."

His round face colored. "Look, all I'm saying is that

there are a lot of things we don't understand. You can't tell; this might be one of them."

He was right. There were many things around us we don't understand or comprehend, but as far as I was concerned, a Martian spaceman with a head the size of a watermelon and who lived three hundred of our years wasn't one of them. "You're right, Jack" was all I said.

As we pulled up in front Marvin Lewis' place, a flake of snow struck the windshield.

Jack grunted. "Good thing I bought a heavier coat."

With a grin, I glanced at him and eyed his rotund body. "You don't have anything to worry about. You got plenty of insulation even without the coat. It's guys like me with no meat on their bones that have to worry."

He muttered a curse. "You skinny guys always say stuff like that. I'll have you know, I get just as cold as you do and just as fast."

A sharp gust of wind hit the Silverado, rocking it.

"You staying out here or going inside? We can leave the engine running."

He waved my suggestion off. "I'll go inside."

Marvin Lewis heard us drive up, and as we hurried through the light snowfall to his porch, he opened the door and screen.

"Hurry up, boys!" he shouted, holding the screen open for us. "Go on into the kitchen. It's warm in there," he said as we hurried past him.

I sniffed the sweet, full aroma of baking cookies or cake. "Something smells good."

He laughed as he closed the door. "Cookies. Fix them ever' once in a while for the grandkids—actually, they're great-great-grandkids. They stay here after school until their mother picks them up." He led the way into the kitchen. "They're good company for an old codger like me." He gestured to the table. "Sit." He opened the oven door, and the warm, rich smell reminded me of my childhood back in Church Point.

My mother, Leota, was an orphan, so when she and my old man married, they lived with my grandparents. Mama Ola loved to cook and bake. That's where my mother picked up the finer points of baking. About once a week Mama Ola baked up a heaping batch of cookies. I could smell them as soon as I climbed off the school bus a quarter mile down the lane.

Without asking, Marvin set cups and coffeepot on the table. "Pour your own. I need to take out the cookies, or they'll burn."

After stacking most of them on a platter, he placed several of them in a chipped plate and set it on the table before us. "One of my biggest sins," he said, seating himself and pouring a cup of steaming coffee, "is dunking sugar cookies in coffee."

I took a bite. He was right. Anything that good had to be sinful.

"So," he asked after his first bite, "what can I do for you? I figured you'd be headed back to Austin by now."

"Just about ready. By the way, do you know anyone around here who drives a white car, a small one, maybe a Honda?"

The white brows over his blue eyes knit in a frown. He scratched his head. "Not right offhand. Why?"

So it was Taggart. "Just curious. I've seen one around, but I didn't recognize the driver. Figured it might be some-one who knew Justin."

For a moment, the twinkle in his eyes vanished. "Might be some of those who live up the road at Woodbine, com-muting to work."

"That's probably it," I replied, dropping the subject.

"I heard you was with Harlan when he had his heart attack."

"Yeah." I went back over the same story I had told the sheriff. "He said he'd seen the spaceman."

"Yeah," Jack put in. "He really believed there was one out there."

Marvin laughed. "He told me too. I don't think so. I believe the man is still buried out there somewhere in the cemetery. Probably nothing but dust by now."

Jack glanced at me. I cleared my throat. "You're proba-bly right. Wouldn't it be a surprise for your mayor if the bones were found?"

The older man frowned. "What do you mean?"

"That mayor who wrote the letter to the newspaper. Houston—the guy who left Elysian Hills and no one heard from again. I figure he'd really be surprised."

A wary look momentarily replaced the twinkle in his eyes. "I imagine he would."

After taking another bite of dunked cookie, I said, "Makes you wonder why he went to Chicago and why he never came back. I guess it was because his wife left."

"I suppose so." His tone was noncommittal.

"From what folks in town say, you must have been the last one to talk to him when you bought his land."

The wizened old man smiled and nodded. "Reckon I could have been. Jim Bob just wanted to get shed of it, and since he owed me for a previous loan, I just paid him the difference."

I sipped my coffee. "How many acres?"

"Six sections."

My eyes widened. "Six sections. Close to four thousand acres. Must run a bunch of beef."

He shook his head. "I sold some to Gus and Buck. I was getting up in years and didn't want to bother looking after that much."

I grinned. "I can understand that."

At that moment, the front door burst open, and a young voice shouted, "We're here, PawPaw!"

"In the kitchen, kids." He grinned up at me. "The kids."

Bundled against the dropping temperatures, a boy of about ten entered, leading a younger girl by the hand. They stared at Jack and me shyly as Marvin introduced us. But as soon as he pointed to the cookies on the cabinet, their shyness fled.

Marvin accompanied us to the door. "You fixing to head back to Austin?"

"As far as I know, unless the family wants me to do anything else."

He frowned. "What would that be?"

I shrugged. "Who knows?" I offered my hand. "You take care, you hear?"

After we pulled back onto the highway, Jack said, "We're not really leaving, are we?"

"I won't know until we see what's in that camera," I replied, indicating the disposable between us on the seat.

* * *

On the outskirts of Fort Worth in a suburb named Haltom City, we found a pharmacy that offered one-hour film developing. We waited next door at a McDonald's. Jack put away three Big Macs, a Diet Coke, and an apple pie. I had a coffee. I was still full from Lewis' sugar cookies.

Sitting in the pickup an hour later, I took the envelope of pictures and quickly thumbed through them. I paused at the exposure made of the open casket.

"Well," said Jack, "what is it? Huh?"

I studied the shot a few moments, noting the crook in the left femur, then handed it to Jack. "Take a look. The left leg."

"Jeez" was all he could mutter.

Slowly nodding, I replied, "Yeah. That's Jim Bob Houston. I'd bet anything." I studied the snapshots another few moments and added, "And you can clearly see there are no extra bones in there." I handed Jack the picture. "See what I mean?"

"I see," he muttered. Then Jack looked up at me with a puzzled frown. "I wonder . . . Does that mean the spaceman wasn't killed? That he's alive, like Barton claimed? Or that he never existed except in the minds of the good people of Elysian Hills?"

I shrugged. "I'll go along with the latter. They just made him up."

Jack paused, a curious frown on his face. "Or maybe he had no bones, just a sort of ectoplasm."

"Ectoplasm?"

"You know, sort of a jellylike stuff. He could have just dissolved in there."

All I could do was shake my head. "Come on, Jack."

"Well, it could be," he retorted, handing me the picture.

"So, now what?" His lips parted as another thought struck him. "Hey, you don't suppose—you don't suppose that Justin Chester knew about this, do you? The bones, I mean."

"How could he? All he knew was what Barton told him, that the spaceman wasn't in the grave."

Jack frowned. "I don't know. I—"

I held up a hand. "Hold on. Let me ramble a minute." I paused, trying to shape my thoughts. "I don't think he had any idea Houston was buried there. Justin discovered the location of the grave and was determined to dig it up. Some- one in Elysian Hills had to learn that Barton and Chester had found the site of the grave. And that someone knew it was only a matter of time until Justin would exhume the casket. They couldn't let him do that, so they had to stop him. They struck him on the back of his head hard enough to kill him and made the car wreck look like an accident." I drew a deep breath. "Well? What do you think?"

"Can you prove it?" he asked, looking at me.

"No," I said. "But if it happened that way, I will."

"Hold on. If Barton knew who was in the grave, why didn't he tell Justin?"

For a moment, I pondered his question. "Remember when Harlan started out the back door? He made the remark that maybe he should have told Justin, but he didn't know how far he could trust him. You remember that?"

Slowly, Jack nodded. "Yeah. Yeah. I remember that."

"That's why."

Chapter Twenty-one

By the time we reached our motel on the outskirts of Reuben, the snow was falling more heavily. We hurried into our room and turned on the heater.

Jack pulled out a fifth of Jim Beam from his suitcase and held it up. "Too cold for beer. Want a drink?"

I did, but now wasn't the time. I wanted to keep my head clear while I put together my thoughts on who might have killed not only Justin Chester, but also Jim Bob Houston.

Jack poured a large drink, splashed a tad of water into it from the tap, and crawled onto his bed to watch TV. I pulled out my notes and laid them out on the table.

Then I thought about the three sheets of paper I'd taken from Justin's "safe." While Jack watched TV, I went downstairs and copied the three pages, rolled them up, and, once back upstairs, deposited them into my briefcase.

Now I had copies.

I pulled out a blank pad and began writing.

The only absolute certainty I had was that the spaceman, if there were one, was not in his grave. And I felt with as much certainty that the bones in the grave were those of Jim Bob Houston.

From then on, all was conjecture.

My day had been busy, but I had not learned as much of Perry and Ford as I did about Houston and his wife. Tomorrow I'd try to learn more—casually, of course.

I wondered about Jim Bob Houston's wife. Had they divorced? Or was she now a widow? And where was she?

And if the bones were those of Houston, then who set up the trust funds Mabel had mentioned for needy individuals in Chicago?

A blast of cold air slammed against the window. I paused, lifting my gaze and peering through the motel walls in the direction of the Diablo Canyons behind Harlan Barton's place, shivering as I imagined the intensity of the cold out there tonight. Slowly I shook my head, going back to another question that continued to nag at me. If Barton knew that Jim Bob was in the grave, why didn't he go the police?

The only explanation I could come up with was that Sheriff Perry was part of the murder scheme with Buck Ford. That would explain why he denied knowing Justin Chester, the sloppy accident report, and why Ford lied about the pickup in the creek. As far as motive, both men had the same: to prevent the discovery of Jim Bob Houston's body.

Leaning back in the chair, I stretched my arms over my head, a jumble of thoughts ricocheting off the insides of my skull. I thought of my boss, Marty, and suddenly his admonition to learn everything about everyone flashed into my head.

For the next hour, I tried to run down even one of the alleged trusts set up by Jim Bob Houston. Mabel Hooker had said they were for needy individuals, but, try as I could, I found no evidence of any trust in the Chicago area endowed by Jim Bob Houston.

Frustrated, I gave up, turning my attention to local land records. Houston had sold his land before he disappeared. Marvin Lewis in turn sold portions of the land to Gus Perry and Buck Ford. Maybe I could find something there.

Digital technology is an amazing time-saver if the information is available. Availability. That's the key, but in Montague County, Texas, where Elysian Hills deeds were filed and maintained, public records were only available digitally since 1992. Prior records had to be looked up the old-fashioned way, by hand.

Larger counties in the state, such as Bexar or Dallas or Tarrant or Harris, have public records online back into the eighties, but that's because, with a larger tax base, they can afford to have the records copied.

I glanced at my watch. Almost eleven. Fully dressed, Jack lay snoring on his bed. The back of my neck was stiff. I massaged the stiffness from it, then contacted Eddie Dyson for all the financial records he could find for Jim Bob Houston in Illinois.

During the night, the snow stopped falling, leaving only a couple of inches. Next morning, I stood at the window, staring out over the white landscape beyond the parking lot as the sun rose, a red ball on a solid black horizon. A white Honda passed before my eyes, and by the time I threw open the door, it had exited the parking lot.

Was that Taggart? And if it were, what was he after?

Early risers clogged the motel restaurant, filling it with the buzz of conversation. We found a table by a window near the rear of the restaurant and ordered.

Sipping our coffee while waiting for our order, we discussed the events of the last few days. "How do we find out if that skeleton is definitely Houston, Tony? If you don't trust Sheriff Perry, can't we just turn it over to some other county or city official?"

"What will they do? It's out of their jurisdiction, and, believe me, it's a toss-up as to which is more important to a cop, jurisdiction or Sunday afternoon football."

He chuckled.

The waitress placed steaming plates before us. I had scrambled eggs, sausage, and toast. Jack—well, he had a Jack-sized platter of eggs, bacon, sausage, and pancakes.

I much prefer sunny beaches and skimpy bikinis to chilling snow and bundled snow bunnies, but the drive later that morning to Elysian Hills provided spectacular scenery, rolling hills covered with a blanket of pristine snow, the sun reflecting off it like millions of glistening diamonds.

Once, at the edge of a thicket, we spotted two deer grazing. The buck looked up as we passed, his big-eyed gaze following us until we were out of sight.

"Yeah, this is pretty, but it's too flat for me," Jack muttered. "Give me rocky hills and tall pines." He grew silent, then, after a few moments, asked, "What's on the agenda this morning?"

"Montague and then Mabel Hooker."

"Montague?" He frowned. "What's that? Sounds like some kind of sickness."

I shook my head in despair. "The county seat. I want to look at some deeds."

"Deeds?"

"Yeah. Land deeds."

After that, I had a few questions I wanted to ask Mabel Hooker.

Montague was a small town in the middle of the Post Oak Savannah of North Texas. Graceful Corinthian columns with Doric capitals supported the gabled porticos of the three-story, redbrick courthouse. As in many of the rural courthouses of the twenties and thirties, the second floor was really the main floor, the lower level being called the basement, although there were windows peering outside.

I didn't know exactly what I was looking for. I suppose some evidence of collusion and conspiracy between the sheriff and Buck Ford.

We parked in front and took the sidewalk that led to the steep flight of steps to the main entrance.

Our first stop would be the tax office, where, after studying a plat of Elysian Hills to locate the property, I obtained a legal description, and with that description, the county clerk's office could point me to the deed-record books in which the deeds were filed.

The books, two feet by two feet and each clothbound with leather spines, lined the wall.

I had gone through this same process in the past in Travis County. My first experience left me in awe at the detailed records maintained by the county. An experienced eye can take a piece of property and trace its ownership all the way back to the days of Spanish land grants.

In less than fifteen minutes, I found the deed between Marvin William Lewis and Jim Bob Houston dated November 23, 1985.

The deed stated that Lewis paid Houston $100,000.00 for six sections of land and mineral rights. The signatures at the bottom of the document were notarized by Pearl Ragsdale, P.O. Box 749, Elysian Hills, Texas, 76251-4963, on November 23, 1985. I glanced at the filing date. March 12, 1986.

I paid little attention to the time between the signing of the contract and the filing of the deed. There's always a lapse of time between the two. Of course, almost five months seemed unusual, but I reminded myself that out here in rural Texas, time didn't mean as much as in metropolitan Texas.

The next few pages were the deeds for the sale of the sections to Buck Ford and Gus Perry for $40,000.00 each in June of 1986. I studied the documents, noting that Lewis paid $250 an acre and sold it for a little over $320 an acre, which meant he picked up 1,280 acres for $20,000. Around $160 an acre. Not a bad move, even back in eighty-five.

In a way, I had to admire the old man. Three-twenty was more than a fair price. He could have gotten four hundred on the open market.

Paying the clerk a nominal fee, I made copies of the documents.

We paused by the front doors to bundle up against the cold. Through the frosty windows I spotted a white Honda driving slowly along the street. I shoved the door open and ran onto the porch, but the Honda turned south and disappeared behind a row of businesses.

By the time we reached the outskirts of Montague, snow had melted from the highways. The rolling hills on either side were beginning to show patches of brown.

Jack cleared his throat. "Did you find anything back there that will help? Deeds and that legal stuff are all Greek to me."

I squeezed the steering wheel until my knuckles turned white. "I don't think so. It all looks perfectly legal to me."

Chapter Twenty-two

I had two individuals I was focusing on—Buck Ford and Sheriff Gus Perry—and to tell the truth, nothing I had discovered implicated either man in anything. In fact, I'd discovered nothing to incriminate anyone in a court of law.

All I had was the business transaction between Marv Lewis and Jim Bob Houston, and then between Lewis and Perry and Ford, respectively, all perfectly legal as far as I could see. I was at a dead end.

The notary who had witnessed the contract was deceased. I had no legal recourse to access the notary's files, and even if I did, I knew I would find no improprieties.

Nope, I told myself. I'd struck out on the land transactions.

I headed back to Elysian Hills to see Mabel Hooker. I wasn't certain just how to approach her. Since I had no evidence of murder, and I couldn't mention the skeleton in the grave without stirring up maybe more trouble than I

172

wanted, I decided to see if I could finesse some answers from her, a skill in which I admit I had never been very successful.

Mabel Hooker smiled broadly when we hurried in from the cold. "You're getting to be regular customers, boys."

Jack popped the tab on a can of Dr. Pepper while I poured some coffee. "Friendly town."

Her ruddy face beamed. "Always has been."

"By the way," I said, sitting in a worn chair. "Jim Bob Houston's wife, Sara Ann. Any idea where she went?"

"Sara Ann?" She looked at me in surprise. "For heaven's sake, that was over twenty years ago." The surprise on her face faded into a suspicious frown. "What do you need her for?"

I lied. "I have a writer friend who's interested in your town. Thought she might do a couple of articles about it. I was lining up folks for her to interview after she talked to you business people."

She must have believed me, for she shook her head. "I don't know where she went when she left here, but last Christmas when I went shopping over at Henrietta, just this side of Wichita Falls, I ran into her. She remarried several years after she left here and settled in Henrietta. Name's Rawlings now. I don't remember her husband's given name."

I winked at her. "Thanks. That'll do. My friend can run her down."

Jack had wandered over to a pinball machine and was busy sticking quarters into it.

At that moment, one of Buck Ford's cattle trucks roared past. "I guess Buck Ford is probably one of the most prosperous members of Elysian Hills. I'm always seeing his trucks on the road."

"Yeah." She hooked a thumb over her shoulder in the direction of his spread. "He's always been a go-getter. That's one man who never lets anything keep him from getting what he wants." She chuckled and raised an eyebrow. "Most of the time, that is."

"Most of the time?" I looked at her, curious.

"Yeah. He met his match with Jim Bob. A couple years before Jim Bob disappeared, him and Buck Ford had a big falling out. Cattle and land argument. Houston sued Ford. Got a judgment for a hundred thousand. Ford's business started going downhill, but he managed to hold on."

The word *motive* flashed before my eyes like a shooting star. I nodded in the direction of Ford's feedlots. "Doesn't look like he has any problems now."

"He don't. In fact, he wasn't hurting none when he bought those two sections from Marvin, though I never could figure out why Marvin sold them to him."

I nodded. "I remember you said there was some kind of family problem, wasn't it?"

"Yep." She shrugged. "But old Marv, he knows how to make a dollar, so he sold the sections to Buck. And Buck ain't no fool. Then when the oil and gas hit—" She shook her head and whistled. "Well, sir, it took off big-time. I suppose old Buck is probably a millionaire a couple times over."

I couldn't help thinking to myself, *even if it meant murdering someone.*

"Truth is," she added, "the sheriff isn't no slouch. He

runs a few hundred head of prime Black Angus. Studs his
bulls for a nice fee. And he's got a few wells."

On impulse after leaving Mabel's, I took Cemetery Road.

Jack frowned at me. "You going back to the cemetery,
Tony?"

"Nope. Thought I'd stop by Barton's place."

"What for?" He knit his eyebrows.

"Just to look around."

A sly grin erased his frown. "You mean to see if you
can find that stuff we were looking for a couple days ago."

I glanced at him and nodded. "Yeah. I got to thinking.
You know, one side of the barn caved in. Maybe a second
seed bin is under that part of the barn."

He remained silent for a few moments. As we approached
the old bridge, he said, "You starting to believe there is a
spaceman?"

Rolling my eyes, I looked around at him in exasperation.
"No way, no time, no how."

When we turned onto the dirt drive, the back end of the
Silverado skidded from side to side as the tires slipped in
the mud. I pulled around the house and parked in back, out
of sight from any vehicles passing in front. I stared at the
dilapidated structure some thirty yards distant. The narrow
lane leading to the barn under a canopy of trees was covered with snow.

Climbing out, I headed for the barn with Jack on my heels.
A few tracks dotted the snow—raccoon, rabbit, coyote.

There were several small piles of snow in the barn, having fallen through gaps in the roof. Jack remained outside

while I searched, moving gingerly around fallen timbers. I came up with the same result: nothing.

From outside, Jack called out, "Tony, come take a look at this!"

He stood beside a smooth stretch of snow in the shade of some overhanging elms, pointing to a series of melting tracks. "What made these?"

Now, I've spent a great deal of time outdoors. I can recognize tracks from muskrat to bobcat, but I had never seen any like those marks. They were about eight inches in length. I was struck by their similarity in shape to a tadpole—a tiny tail at the rear of a round body. Whatever they were, they weren't animal tracks.

A few feet on, the snow ended, and the trail, if indeed it was a trail, was lost in the thin mud.

"So? What do you think made them?"

All I could do was shrug. "Beats me. Tumbleweeds? Blowing trash? Whatever."

He gestured at them. "You see where they're headed?" Without giving me a chance to reply, he said, "The Diablo Canyons."

I laughed, and his round face turned red. "Look, Jack," I explained, "any of a number of things could have made those marks." I pointed to a snow-covered tumbleweed lodged in a rusty fence. "Like I said, the wind blowing a tumble-weed, a—"

Before I could continue, he snorted, waved a hand at me to shut up, and stormed back to the Silverado. "Forget it," he said over his shoulder.

* * *

Back at the motel, I booted up my laptop as Jack headed for the door. "I'm going to pick up some beer and snacks," he said. "Back in a few minutes."

Nodding briefly, I scanned the screen, excited to see that Eddie's reply was waiting.

In June 1986, Jim Bob Houston deposited $100,000 in the Chicago Mercantile Bank. Over the next two years, there was little activity in the account other than what looked like withdrawals for the usual living expenses. Houston's address on his bank account was 355 Ridge Avenue in Evanston. In 1988, the account was closed. And Jim Bob Houston dropped out of sight.

Leaning back, I studied the information. Not much. The transactions easily could have been handled by mail. I Googled a map of Evanston and searched for the address on Ridge Avenue.

It popped up, complete with telephone number.

I couldn't help thinking that, whether we like it or not, Big Brother is here, peeking over our shoulder. As digital technology continues to expand, less and less of our personal business will remain private. Even today, there is little I could not learn of any individual if I were willing to spend the time and money.

Having no idea whom I was calling, I dialed the Evanston number. On the third ring, a woman answered. "Talley Apartments. Nora Talley speaking."

I introduced myself and explained that I was trying to run down a man who had lived there from 1986 through 1988.

I was expecting a dead end, but to my surprise, she replied,

"I've been here forty years and seen a lot of faces. What was his name?"

My hopes surged. I couldn't believe my luck. "Houston. Jim Bob Houston."

"What year did you say?"

I repeated the years.

"Hold on a minute," she replied, placing the receiver on a table.

Several minutes passed before she returned. "Sorry to keep you waiting, Mr. Boudreaux, but Homer—he was my husband—Homer kept up with everyone who rented an apartment from us. He kept them in spiral notebooks by the year. We have—" she hesitated, then continued. "We have a three-story brick with rooms that we rent out to single men. Some of them have been with us since we opened in sixty-one. I run the place now. Been running it since 1988, when Homer died."

"I'm sorry."

"That's how the good Lord planned life. The good with the bad. Homer, he was a good man." She paused. When she replied, her voice was tentative. "That Houston man is in our book. He stayed in B-14 beginning in March of eighty-six. That's a basement room at the front of the house." She hesitated and then with a sense of urgency continued. "Yes, I remember that one. Homer and me always wondered about him."

"Oh? Why is that?" I crossed my fingers.

I wanted to shout with joy when she replied, "He traveled a lot. He was never there. We saw him when he rented the room, and then two or three times a year afterward." She paused, then, her tone suggesting embarrassment, explained,

"All the rooms had radiators. We adjusted them twice a year. There were always clothes and toilet articles in his room. Sometimes nothing was disturbed for months." She hastened to add, "Not that I was snooping, but I had to let exterminators and those sorts of people in."

"Hey, I understand."

She continued. "According to Homer's book, Houston moved out in August of 1988. That was the month before Homer died. Heart attack. I've kept the books ever since."

"I know it's been a long time, Mrs. Talley, but if I sent you a picture of him, do you think you might be able to identify him?"

She hesitated. "I don't know. Eighty-eight. That's twenty years ago."

"But could you try? If you have e-mail, I can send it to you."

"I'll try, but I can't promise nothing."

She gave me her e-mail address. I thanked her and hung up.

Now all I needed were pictures of Gus Perry and Buck Ford circa 1980 or so.

Chapter Twenty-three

I glanced at my watch. Just after three. Picking up the morning copy of *The Reuben Journal*, I noted it had been established in 1959, which meant they had archives well prior to the eighties. I grabbed the phone book and jotted down the address for the *Journal*.

That's where I might find my twenty-year-old pictures.

I met Jack coming in with the beer and snacks as I was leaving. "Back in a few minutes," I said, brushing past him.

"But—"

I ignored him.

After explaining to the receptionist at the *Journal* that I was doing historical articles on Elysian Hills, I followed her back to the paper's archives.

Fifteen minutes later, I had mid-1980s pictures of Perry, Ford, and, for good measure, Jim Bob Houston, copied to a portable USB drive.

Thirty minutes later, the three shots were whizzing through cyberspace to dtalley@ev.rr.tag.

And five minutes later, she replied that she did not recognize any of the men.

Stunned, I stared at her message.

I opened my cell and called her.

"I'm sorry," she replied, "but none of them looked familiar. I have a good memory for faces. Those three were just too young."

A tiny thought ignited in the back of my head. "How old was he? Any idea?"

She hesitated. "I'd guess in his late sixties."

Thanking her, I hung up.

"Bad news, huh?"

I glanced at Jack. "Not good."

He grimaced. "Sorry."

Puzzled, I tried to revise my theory. The only good thing to come from her answer was that Jim Bob Houston had not rented the apartment on Ridge Avenue in Evanston. That meant the likelihood of the skeleton's being Houston's was even a greater possibility.

Gazing into space, I considered various possibilities.

I was convinced Ford and Perry were involved.

Ford had lied about the pickup, and Perry had denied knowing Justin.

And then, Harlan Barton swore he had seen two men burying something in the spaceman's grave. Later, he dug up the grave, saw whoever was inside, but did not report what he had witnessed to the local law. Why?

To me the only logical explanation still was that the local law was involved. I remembered the somber remark of Harlan

Barton. *"On the surface, Elysian Hills looks like a simple lit-tle community, but there is a dark side that not many ever see."*

I had a chilling feeling that I was stumbling into the dark side of Elysian Hills.

Ford and Perry, I reminded myself, could have hired someone to play the part of Jim Bob Houston. Even as I considered the idea, I realized its drawbacks outweighed the advantages.

Who could they hire to play the role of Jim Bob Houston two or three times a year? And wouldn't that individual be mighty curious as to what was going on? They couldn't have hired anyone locally, for he would have known Jim Bob.

The more I considered the situation, the more confused I became.

As much as I hate to admit it, sometimes I seem to live in a permanent state of confusion. I've never had the capabil-ity to cut to the heart of the matter succinctly.

Usually I blunder ahead, making one mistake after an-other. Unlike Al Grogan, one of my co-workers at Blevins Security, I always struggle to put together logical step-by-step deductions to arrive at a valid solution.

To compensate, I figure if I keep plodding ahead, sooner or later, I'll find what I'm seeking. After all, a person can't be wrong all the time. And all I needed was to be right that one time.

Jack grunted. "Stuck?"

Keeping my gaze on the laptop, I nodded. "Big-time."

"Well," he drawled, "read back over everything. Maybe something will ring a bell."

I arched an eyebrow in skepticism, but after a few mo-ments, I shrugged. What the heck? It couldn't hurt.

An hour later, I leaned back and rubbed my burning eyes. I pushed back from the computer and grabbed my tweed jacket. "I'm going to get some fresh air. Maybe a cup of coffee and pie."

Jack raised an eyebrow and grinned. "Don't get lost."

The cold air was bracing, its sharpness filling my lungs and clearing my head. The glittering stars seemed even more vibrant in the frigid night. Hands jammed in my pockets, I paced the galleries around the building, pondering my situation.

Thinking I might buy a lottery ticket since I'd had no luck on my scratch-off tickets, I ambled over to the Valero truck stop where a dozen or so rigs idled while their drivers put themselves around a hot meal.

As I passed in front of a rumbling Freightliner, a voice from the darkness between two of the giant rigs stopped me. "Hey, mister."

I looked around as a slight figure in threadbare clothes looked up at me.

"You spare a couple bucks?"

His battered fedora was pulled down over his eyes. A couple of weeks' worth of whiskers covered his sepulcher-thin face, and the stench of unwashed body emanated from him even in the frigid air.

I peered into the shadows covering his face. There was something familiar about him. "Sure. What's your name?"

He held out a bony hand. "John."

I caught my breath and whispered. "Boudreaux? John Roney Boudreaux?"

He froze and stared up at me. "Who are you? I ain't done nothing." He started to back away.

"Don't you recognize me, John? It's me. Tony. Tony Boudreaux. I'm your son."

He just stared at me. The fear faded from his eyes. He nodded. "I remember. Yeah, yeah, I remember good, boy."

The few times I'd run into my old man in the last few years, he'd never stayed around long. He was like the *feu-follet,* the Cajun fairy darting through the swamps, here one moment, gone the next. Last I saw him was in Austin, where he pilfered a statue of the goddess Diana from Danny O'Banion and hocked it.

"How have you been?"

Relaxing, he cackled. "Still staying ahead of them, boy. Like they say, maintaining my character by staying one step ahead of the law."

I looked around, then spotted the restaurant. "You gotta be hungry. How about something to eat?"

Fortunately, the restaurant was not crowded. We found a table in a corner away from most of the other customers. He was my father in name only, having deserted us when I was a child. Consequently, when I did meet him, I never could bring myself to call him Father.

He ordered two hamburgers and a beer. I ordered one hamburger and a coffee.

As he sat hunched over the table, stuffing food into his mouth, I simply watched. What do you say when your father rides the rails and bums quarters on street corners for Thunderbird wine or Listerine mouthwash?

More than once I'd asked him to stay with me, told him I would help him start over, but invariably he'd vanish, and usually with whatever items of mine he could pawn.

"I have a room here at the motel. You want to spend the night? Be nice and warm."

He looked up at me from under the battered brim of his fedora, his eyes wary like those of a mouse waiting for the cat to pounce. He shrugged. "I don't care."

"Good. It's settled, then."

I took another bite of hamburger and a swallow of coffee and signaled our waitress for the bill.

Suddenly the loudspeaker called my name, asking me to see the clerk at the cash register for a phone call. I fished a twenty from my wallet and handed it to my old man. "Give this to the waitress. I'll be right back."

It was Jack on the phone. "I hoped I'd catch you down there. How about bringing me a couple hamburgers?"

I rolled my eyes. Where did he put it all? "Okay." I replaced the receiver and headed back to my table.

I hesitated at the dining room door. My old man had disappeared. I glanced at the restroom as I slid into my chair. The unpaid check lay on the table. The remainder of my hamburger had also disappeared.

Moments later, the waitress returned. "Cash or credit, sir?" she asked sweetly.

I frowned. "What about the man who was here?"

"Oh, he left." She pointed to the side door. "He said you'd take care of the bill."

I stared up at her in disbelief, and then I started laughing. My old man had gotten me again. "All right," I said. "But put two more hamburgers on there, will you please? I'll take them with me."

A few minutes later, I stepped out into the frigid air. I

looked up and down the interstate, wondering which way John Roney Boudreaux had fled this time and where he would spend such a cold night.

A strange sense of disappointment came over me. At first I couldn't figure out why, but as I stared into the darkness, I knew the answer. In my own way, I loved the old man, but I sure would have liked to kick his scrawny rear. Even if I did, I knew I'd never be able to convince him of what he was missing. "Take care, old man," I muttered.

Chapter Twenty-four

Before returning to my room, I circled the parking lot, searching for a white Honda. There were none.

I turned the case over in my mind while I showered. Dora Talley had not recognized any of the three pictures I sent her. She claimed the man posing as Jim Bob Houston was older, in his sixties. That was twenty years or so ago, which would put him in his eighties or even early nineties now, I told myself.

The only person around that age still alive in Elysian Hills was Marvin Lewis. Impossible. It was probably another elderly member of the community who had long since passed on. Still, I needed to check both theories out. I shook my head and climbed into bed, but sleep refused to come. Marvin Lewis was too much on my mind.

More than once I've had all my neat little theories blow up in my face like a string of Fourth of July firecrackers. When that happened, it was usually because I had unconsciously been guiding the direction of the investigation, placing neat little theories into precise little slots where they didn't belong. And if they refused to fit, I pounded them in. With results not surprising.

Flipping on the bedside light, I rolled out of bed and padded over to the desk. Behind me, Jack groaned and rolled over. I heard the covers snap over his head.

Pulling out my note cards, I started from the beginning.

Each time I ran across a card with information I thought might be a backbreaker, I put it aside.

The first one was Sheriff Perry's denial of knowing Justin; the second was Buck Ford's claim that he saw the pickup in the creek; the next was Barton's assertion that he had seen two men digging in the cemetery that night twenty years ago.

I asked myself the same question I'd asked a dozen times. Why didn't the old man report it to the sheriff? And for the twelfth time, I came up with the same answer. The sheriff was one of the two.

Then I turned to the cards recording Houston's land sale to Marvin Lewis, who subsequently sold part of the property to Ford and Perry. I wasn't an abstract-of-title man but I could see nothing suspicious in the transaction.

I glanced at the photocopies of the document on file in the Montague County Courthouse. The contract was legal. Were it not, it could not have been filed.

Every crime possesses three factors: motive, opportunity, and means.

If indeed Barton had seen Buck Ford and the sheriff at the cemetery twenty or so years earlier, their current motives were obvious. They believed that Justin was planning on exhuming the coffin. They knew what he would find when he opened the casket. They had no choice but to shut him up permanently.

As far as Marvin Lewis went, I could see no motive. He believed the same as Justin about the UFO, which supported my theory that whomever Nora Talley had met twenty years ago had passed on.

Opportunity? Ford and Perry were in town. Lewis was visiting his family in Gainesville. Another reason to eliminate Lewis.

I decided to send Nora Talley an image of Marvin Lewis. I figured it was a waste of time, but, remembering Marty's assertion not to leave out anything about anybody, I knew I had to cover all my bases. Once she failed to recognize him, I could dismiss him from my list of suspects and start digging for a third member of the triad that murdered Justin.

Jack groaned sleepily as I opened the door early the next morning. "What's going on?"

"I'm running down to the newspaper. I'll meet you in the restaurant in thirty minutes or so. Order me coffee and a small stack of pancakes."

Within minutes at the news office, I found what I was looking for and headed back. A red Blazer had taken my parking spot, so I was forced to park around the corner of the motel from our room.

In the restaurant, Jack was wading through a platter of pancakes, eggs, sausage, and hash browns. That man loved to eat.

When I finished a few minutes later, he was still shoveling it in, so I left him behind while I went upstairs to e-mail the image of Marvin Lewis to Nora Talley. "A waste of time,"

I muttered as I clicked the insert, attach, and send commands. But I had to try.

Thirty minutes later, when I opened the door and stepped out onto the second-floor gallery, I spotted a white Honda turning onto the access road. I hurried to the rail and leaned over as far as I could. The driver was male, but his features were too vague. Taggart? I wondered.

The parking lot was wet with melted snow when we pulled out. "What's up today?"

"Henrietta."

"Who's she?"

Driving slowly onto the access road, I laughed and headed for the underpass that would take us to the FM Road 1287 leading to Elysian Hills. I noticed the brakes were a little spongy but thought nothing of it.

"This one's no she. It's a town. About forty miles west of here. Just this side of Wichita Falls."

"What's there?"

"Jim Bob Houston's ex-wife. I figured I'd see what kind of information I can get from her."

Once we hit the winding farm-to-market road, I kicked the Silverado up to fifty-five. The sun was bright, and the road was drying quickly. I adjusted the rearview mirror to keep the sun from my eyes.

"Must be a busy day out at Ford's," I remarked as the sixth cattle truck whizzed past, heading for the interstate. We topped the crest of a hill and in the distance spotted a school bus heading in the same direction as we. Beyond the bus were two more cattle rigs heading toward us.

Jack looked around at me. "That Ford guy, he's got some operation, huh?"

"Yeah. Some operation," I replied, watching the approaching rigs growing larger.

They passed the school bus just as it slowed and flashed yellow lights and then red lights.

Without warning, one rig swerved into my lane, then jerked back abruptly. I swung to the right and hit my brakes.

The pedal slammed to the floor. I pumped frantically, but the brakes were gone, and I found myself trying to hold on to a two-thousand-pound pickup slamming through mud and bear grass at fifty miles an hour toward a stopped school bus.

My only choice was to cut to the right and smash through a three-strand barbed-wire fence, coming to rest in the middle of a pasture, hub deep in mud.

The two rigs pulled off the road, and while one driver hurried to the bus, the other waded through the mud to us, apologizing profusely. "The sun got in my eyes, stranger. Man, I'm sorry. I'll call for road service and tell my boss, Buck Ford."

"Okay. Call Newt Gibons in Elysian Hills."

He looked at me, puzzled. "You ain't from around here."

"No, but I know Newt."

He shrugged. "You got it."

The driver at the bus waved that all was fine. Moments later, a young boy came racing up the lane and climbed aboard. The bus pulled away.

Newt Gibons shook his head and pursed his lips. "I ain't got no chain long enough to haul you out of here." He looked around, scratching his head and eyeballing the set of tracks in the mud. "You did a bang-up job, I'll say that," he drawled.

At that moment, the steady pounding of a powerful engine

interrupted us. A man on a red tractor was rolling up the lane. He rounded the corner of the pasture, eyed the damage I'd done to the fence, then drove over to us.

Newt held up a hand. "Howdy, Finas."

Then I recognized the old gentleman as one of those with whom I'd spoken at Mabel's my first day in town. I nodded. "Sorry about the fence, Mr. Irvin. Of course, I'll pay for it."

Newt looked at me. "You boys know each other?"

"Sure do. Mr. Irvin there told me where I could find Justin Chester when I first came to town."

The old man shook his head. "Hated to hear about that boy. He might have been a couple points off the compass, but he was a decent man."

I gave him our Austin address so he could bill Blevins Security for the fence, after which he hauled us out with his tractor.

Newt raised the front end. The impact had forced mud and grass into every crevice in the undercarriage of the pickup.

I shook my head. "I can't see a thing except mud."

Newt grunted and gestured to the wrecker. "Hop in. We'll clean it off back at the shop. Then we can get a handle on what happened."

We climbed into his wrecker and headed back to Elysian Hills.

In a wry drawl, he asked, "What happened back there?"

"No idea. I hit the brakes, and they hit the floor."

"Scared the bejezzus out of me," Jack muttered. "I didn't think we were ever going to stop."

Flexing his thin fingers on the steering wheel, Newt grunted. "I figured you would be gone out of here by now."

I ignored the implied question. "You said you knew Jim Bob Houston, didn't you?"

A frown knit his forehead. "Sure. Good man."

"It's hard to believe someone would just up and leave town without saying anything to anyone."

Gibons arched an eyebrow. His tone was thoughtful when he replied. "Never could understand that. Jim Bob grew up here. He was our mayor when he was younger. I'd have given hundred to one odds against that old boy's pulling up stakes and leaving." He paused, then continued. "There was some talk around that Jim Bob had got hisself mixed up with the wrong kind of people, but nothing came of it. Then we heard he was up in Chicago, so the talk must've just been that, talk."

Jack glanced at me. I raised an eyebrow.

"He have any enemies or anything?"

Newt frowned.

Quickly I added, "He had almost four thousand acres, a good cattle and oil business." I shook my head and lapsed into my homespun drawl. "Why leave? It just don't make sense, you know?"

Newt didn't reply. He kept his eyes fixed forward several seconds before replying. "Mighta been his old lady had something to do with it."

Playing the innocent, I replied. "His wife?"

"Yep. They say she played around on him, then up and left. He shook his head. "I don't believe it."

"Oh? Why not?"

He looked around, his blue eyes staring like beacons at me. "Sara wasn't that kind of woman. At least, I didn't think so. Still, one day she just up and flew the coop." He touched his brakes as he pulled across the highway to his shop. "But today, you can't tell about nobody."

I looked over the rolling countryside. "So, Elysian Hills used to be a sizeable town, huh?"

He chuckled. "Way back. Most of the young folks leave now." He nodded in the direction of the cemetery. "Older folks are going pretty fast now. Won't be long there won't be no more than a handful of us left." He pointed to the redbrick house on the hill above the UFO museum. "I reckon old Marv's the oldest one around now. In the last ten years he's lost all his old cronies."

His old cronies! I wondered if any of them could have been the one who rented the apartment in Chicago. It shouldn't be too difficult to run down their names and photos.

Fifteen minutes later, Newt Gibons came over to us by the propane heater, drying his hands on a towel. "Well, I reckon I owe you city boys an apology."

I frowned. "An apology?"

"Yep. I reckoned you two was just lollygagging along and ran off the road, but, believe it or not, I was wrong."

I glanced at Jack. "Yeah? How's that?"

A wry grin played over his lips. "It appears some folks around here must not take kindly to you."

"Huh?" I frowned. "What do you mean by that?"

He held up a short tube. "After I hosed the mud off, I saw that someone had cut your brake line."

Chapter Twenty-five

Jack jumped to his feet. "What? But—But—"

I scarcely heard Jack stuttering and stammering. All I could think of was that white Honda leaving the parking lot just before we climbed into the Silverado. "Taggart," I muttered under my breath.

Newt nodded. "Did a good job too, whoever he is," he muttered wryly. "Cut 'em so they'd break the first time you stomped down hard on the brakes. It'll take a few hours. I can't get to them until after dinner. Probably be ready around three."

"Looks like we'll have to use your car, Jack."

He shrugged. "Fine with me, but how do we get back to Reuben?"

Newt spoke up. "Let me give Buck Ford a call. He's got trucks pulling out regular-like. One of those old boys can give you a lift. I'll park your truck out front when it's ready."

Fifteen minutes later, a bright green Kenworth ground to

a halt in front and blasted the horn. We hurried out. Moments later, we were rocketing along the narrow highway bound for Reuben, a hundred conflicting thoughts bouncing around inside my skull.

I couldn't figure what was going on. If Taggart was the one who'd cut the brake lines, that meant that in all likelihood Vanessa Chester was behind it. But why? There was nothing here for her to gain. Justin's estate had already been divided among the three surviving siblings.

Her involvement made no sense at all.

I was still confused when we reached the motel. We threw our gear into Jack's Cadillac and roared away.

An hour later, we approached the outskirts of Henrietta, a pastoral community perched on a sweeping hill overlooking a long valley to the west, beyond which sprawled Wichita Falls.

There were only four Rawlings in the directory, so within minutes I was speaking with Sara Ann. Since insurance ranks right up there with Greek and Latin as confusing to most people, I decided to be an insurance agent. I explained I had learned her location from Mabel Hooker and that my company had contracted with Universal Life Insurance regarding an insurance policy on her ex-husband.

She lived in a neat little cottage on about a half acre of grassy lawn dotted with giant oaks. The layout might have been from one of those better-living magazines, except the grass needed cutting and the flower beds weeding. On closer observation, the fence needed a coat of paint, and holes pocked the asphalt driveway.

She opened the door before the echoes of the bell faded

away. A vivacious woman in her early seventies, she wore a blue print dress that fell straight from her shoulders. Her short hair was neatly styled. "Mr. Boudreaux? Please. Come in." She bubbled warmth.

I introduced Jack, and we stepped into the neatly kept house and followed her into the living room, where she gestured to a couch behind a coffee table on which sat a silver serving set with steaming coffee and a pile of oatmeal cookies on a platter beside the coffee.

She poured our coffee. "You'll have to excuse Mr. Rawlings for not greeting you, but he's been ill for the last few months."

I shook my head, remembering the unkempt grounds outside. "I'm sorry."

Smiling demurely, she poured her own cup and sat. "That's mighty sweet of you. Now, how can I help you?"

Leaning forward, I smiled warmly. And then I lied. "Mabel Hooker said to tell you hello and to come back for a visit." She nodded, and I continued. "You might not have heard, but sometime after you and Mr. Houston parted ways, he sold his land to Marvin Lewis and just dropped out of sight."

Her eyes grew wide, and her cheeks colored. "Marvin? J. B. sold his land to Marvin Lewis?" She studied me for several moments. I tried but failed to read the meaning of the puzzled amusement in her eyes.

I continued. "You seem surprised."

"I am." She nodded emphatically. "Most surprised that J. B. sold it or anything to Marvin Lewis." She paused, drew a deep breath, then continued. "You see, after I left, I never went back. I never talked to anyone, so I had no idea what was going on. And even if I did, I wouldn't have cared."

Then it hit me. While gossip had it that she had played around with another man, no one knew his identity. Could it have been Marvin Lewis? "Why does it surprise you? I mean, that your husband sold Lewis the land?"

She glanced at Jack, then looked back a me, a defiant gleam in her eyes and a faint smile on her lips. I had the feeling she was debating whether to tell me or not. "Ex-husband, and if you've spoken to anyone in Elysian Hills, then you know I left J. B. Whether I was right or wrong, I don't know. I tried to figure it out for a long time, but Ralph—that's my husband—told me to forget it. It was in the past, and there was nothing I could do to make it right. So I did. I put it behind me. If what I did then was a sin, I'll answer to God when the time comes. I'll have to live with that."

She hesitated. I leaned forward expectantly.

"I've never spoken to anyone about this except my husband." She hesitated, then continued. "Maybe it's time. You see, sometimes our marriage was okay, but more often than not, we were quarreling. J. B. liked women. He wasn't very good at covering up, so naturally I learned about them. After a long, long time, I figured if he could pluck a couple grapes of forbidden fruit, I could do the same. And I did. And when he learned of it, he exploded. That was over twenty years ago." She paused and drew a deep breath. "I've long since stopped slapping blame onto anyone, Mr. Boudreaux. We both made mistakes. Anyway, I left Elysian Hills, signed the divorce papers he sent a few months later, asked for nothing, got the same, and with the exception of Mabel Hooker, I haven't seen anyone from Elysian Hills in all those years."

She paused, her light green eyes fixed on mine. "I know what you're wondering." She continued. "Marvin Lewis. He's the one I had an affair with."

Despite having guessed her lover's identity earlier, my eyes still grew wide. "Marvin Lewis."

"When a woman is angry, Mr. Boudreaux, she isn't too rational. Marvin's wife had been dead a few years, and he was fun to be around. Sure, he was older, but he gave me what J. B. couldn't—companionship, understanding, sympathy. After I left, I was sure the whole story got around town. That's why I was so surprised when you said J.B. sold him the ranch. Either that ex-husband of mine was kicked in the head by a horse, or he signed the papers in his sleep. J. B. never forgave any slight."

"How did J. B. get along with others in town—Buck Ford, Gus Perry, some of them?"

She shrugged. "Fine." She paused and added, "As long as they didn't bother him. Him and Buck Ford got into a big argument one time. J. B. sued Buck and got a judgment. Buck paid it off, but the hard feelings remained—both ways."

I grinned to myself. I had motive. Ford killed Houston. My little theory was right. He and Sheriff Perry were the two men Harlan Barton had seen that night over twenty years ago. They murdered Justin Chester so he could not exhume the spaceman's grave and expose the remains of J. B. Houston.

Sara's forehead knit into a frown. "You said J.B. just dropped out of sight. Anyone ever see him again?"

"Not to my knowledge. He was supposedly living in Chicago, but we can't confirm that."

She pursed her lips. "You think he's dead?"

With a shrug, I lied. "I don't know. He has a twenty-five-thousand-dollar paid-up insurance policy we'd like to get off the books." I hoped she didn't know anything about life insurance. I was stretching credibility like a rubber band, for no insurance company in the world would be eager to pay out any amount just to "get it off the books."

"Is there anything I can do to help?"

I hated lying to her, but I had learned all I could. "No." I shook my head. "We'll just keep digging. Oh, by the way, did Jim Bob have a limp?"

A perplexed frown wrinkled her forehead. "Yes. His left leg. Why?"

"Just for the record, that's all. Just for the record."

Back in the car, Jack grinned at me. "It *is* Houston in the casket."

"Sure looks that way," I replied, closing the door and buckling up.

During the drive back to Reuben, I pondered the information I had garnered. The fact that Marvin Lewis and Sara Houston had had an affair was no reason for Lewis to kill Houston. If anything, the opposite would be true—a headstrong husband flies into a rage and kills his wife's lover.

On the other hand, J. B. Houston and Buck Ford had had a big falling out. Elysian Hills is so desolate. Ford could have killed J. B. anywhere and, with Sheriff Perry's help, buried him in the spaceman's grave. But then a thought that had not occurred to me made me stop and think. What was Perry's motive for helping Ford?

Since Barton had refused to tell the sheriff about Houston's being in the grave, I was convinced Perry was part of the scheme, but exactly what part did he play?

And, I asked myself, how do I prove any of this?

I couldn't. Oh, I could prove Jim Bob was in the grave, but that was it. There was no way I could incriminate Buck Ford or Sheriff Perry. And the truth was, I didn't see any avenue available for me to pursue such a course without some support from the law.

Back in the motel, I plopped down in front of my laptop and all my notes, gathering courage to plunge back in at the very beginning. I had two pieces of evidence. First, the pictures of the crooked femur could match that of Houston, and, second, Houston had never lived in that particular apartment in Chicago. But without Gus Perry's support, I figured I was at a dead end.

Muttering a curse, I pushed myself out of my chair and opened Jack's ice chest for a Budweiser. He said nothing. His raised eyebrows spoke for him.

I held the beer out. "Any objections?"

He laughed. "Hey, I always welcome a partner in sin. That's between you and AA."

I downed three or four icy gulps. Lowering the beer, I grumbled. "Every time I turn around, I hit another dead end."

At that moment, a tiny bell sounded on my laptop, signaling I had mail.

Absently, I plopped down and clicked on the e-mail.

I caught my breath when I spotted a reply from Nora Talley in regard to my morning question.

I opened the mail, and my eyes bulged.

Jack saw the look on my face. "What?"

I read him the response as I stared at the image of Marvin Lewis, some twenty years earlier. Her message said, "'I am certain this is the man who called himself J. B. Houston, and the one I rented the apartment to from March 1986 through December 1988.' Signed, *Nora Talley.*"

So much for my theory about one of Lewis' cronies renting the Chicago apartment.

Chapter Twenty-six

For a moment, I stared at the message, stunned at the obvious implication. Lewis was involved in Houston's death. My brain shifted into high gear. If Lewis had rented the apartment in Houston's name, then he was making an effort to cover up Houston's murder. And the only explanation as to why he would do so was because he was responsible for it in some manner.

Maybe, I told myself, that's why I couldn't figure out exactly what part Perry played in the scheme—because he wasn't part of it. I discarded the idea of Perry's being involved and substituted Marvin Lewis for him. Buck Ford and Marvin Lewis. Still, I couldn't help wondering why Harlan Barton did not go to the sheriff about Houston's grave. Unless Barton knew that Perry had purchased land from Lewis. The two were friends. Maybe the old man figured there might be some unwanted repercussions if he told Perry what he had seen. Maybe.

Then another question popped up. Why the charade? Why try to fabricate two years of Houston's life? What could be gained by that? All good questions, and all without even an inkling of an answer on my part.

Quickly, I pulled out the documents I had copied at the Montague County Courthouse. I had no idea what I was looking for, but Sara Ann's remark about how unbelievable it was that J. B. would sell Marvin Lewis his six sections had stuck with me like bark on one of our green persimmon trees back in Louisiana.

I didn't really know what I was looking for. The records I was studying were twenty years old. I read the notary's name. Pearl Ragsdale, P.O. Box 749, Elysian Hills, Texas, 76251-4963. She had notarized the document in November of 1985. I paused and stared into space. If there were some way I could gain access to her notary journal of 1985, maybe I could—I caught myself. I could what? I could nothing; I would find nothing! Notaries make certain their logs are perfect.

I grimaced and glanced at my watch. Three o'clock. I grabbed my jacket. "Come on, Jack. The truck's bound to be ready."

True to his word, Newt had parked the Silverado in front of his garage. Jack dropped me off and headed back to the motel.

Inside the shop, I gave Newt a credit card. At the same time, I asked, "You remember a woman around here years back by the name of Pearl Ragsdale?"

He looked up at me and grinned, revealing half a dozen missing teeth. "Mama Pearl. Hey, I hadn't thought about her in years. Fine, fine lady." He cocked his head toward the cemetery. "She's buried right down yonder." Then he frowned. "How'd you hear about her?"

"Over in Henrietta. I was doing some insurance work over there, and it just came up. Lady asked me if I knew Pearl. I told her no." I shrugged. "I was just curious."

"Yes, sir. She lived up there just north of Marv Lewis' place. Her and her boy." He tapped his head. "The youngster was slow, but Mama Pearl did everything she could to take care of him. Oliver, that was his name. She was all by her lonesome. Her old man had run off before the kid was born. She did odd jobs around, keeping kids, sewing and patching dresses, paper route—whatever it took to take care of Ollie."

"Sounds like a good woman."

"She was, she was. Somebody got sick, she'd be right there to help." He paused to cut a chunk from his plug of Cannonball chewing tobacco and popped it into his mouth. He offered it to me, but I declined. "And when she took sick, everybody pitched in like she had always done. Wonderful old soul."

I nodded slowly, ready for the story to be over. "What happened?"

With sweeping nonchalance, he replied, "Oh, she died. The cancer. It hit her—" He screwed up his face in concentration. "Let's see. It hit her in eighty-four. Yeah. It was right at Thanksgiving, and we all couldn't eat no more than a couple helpings after hearing the news. She fought it a couple years until around June of eighty-six, I think it was. But she took care of Ollie, her backward boy. Put him in a good home for folks like him down to Fort Worth." He paused to eject a stream of brown juice on the dusty concrete floor. "Dear old soul, she knew she was a goner, and there was no one left to take care of little Ollie." Newt gave me a crooked grin. "That's what we called him hereabouts. He was about forty, I reckon, but he was still little Ollie to us. Anyway, she knew she had to find someplace to put him. She sold her house to Marv Lewis with the provision her and the boy could stay until she died. She must've scraped as hard as she could for the rest of the money. Story is, it cost a heap to keep kids in that home." He shook his head, removed his cap from his bald head, and glanced heavenward. "I just know she's sitting at the right hand of God this moment."

His sincerity touched me. To outsiders, the folks of Elysian Hills might seem country bumpkins, but they were decent human beings trying to live a decent life.

All except a couple of them.

And I was determined to pin their worthless hides to the wall. And then, if I had the chance, to rub some salt into their wounds.

Outside, I sat in my pickup staring at Newt's shop. Mama Pearl intrigued me. Here's a rural woman, left to take care of herself and her son, and she does. Only the good Lord knows how. But how could she have managed to save the funds to put her son in a home like Newt said? The expense had to be outrageous.

On impulse, I made a U-turn and headed back down the road to Sam Fuqua's convenience store.

A wide grin popped onto Sam's face when he spotted me. He nodded. He was busy, so I headed for the coffee, which I carried to the space heater.

After his customers left, he came over. "Hey, man, I didn't figure you'd still be here."

I had a feeling I could trust the older man, but I didn't know how far, so I remained tentative. I asked him about Pearl Ragsdale. He repeated Newt's version of the story.

Sipping my coffee, I muttered, "Wonder what home she sent him to. I've got a nephew in a special home down there somewhere."

He frowned. "It was St. Christopher something, best I remember."

"I heard she lived close to Marvin Lewis."

"Yep. She had a small house about half a mile down the road from Marv. Wasn't much. Her old man hated the sight of work. If he could beg, borrow, or steal enough money for a bottle, he was happier than a hog at the slop trough. The place run down after she died. Bums got to sleeping there. Burned up some years back."

During the drive back to the motel, I ran it all back through my head. Suppose Lewis and Ford killed Houston, buried him in the cemetery, then kept Houston "alive" in Chicago for two years. That way, no one in Elysian Hills would miss J. B. and start asking questions. And if the questions did arise, they would be focused on Chicago, not Elysian Hills.

Even average PIs like me know that in any crime there must be motive, opportunity, and means. Opportunity and means, I didn't worry about. In such a desolate environment, opportunity lurked around every door, and means lay on every tool bench. Motive is what puzzled me.

Land couldn't be the motive, for Lewis had bought it. Then

he turned around and sold two-thirds of it, and one of those thirds to a man he despised, Buck Ford. Of course, being in the murder together, he would not have had much of a choice.

Actually, why would he even buy six sections? He already owned over twelve hundred acres. Unless he was accumulating property to pass on to his children and their children, I reminded myself, remembering his two great-great-grandchildren a few days earlier.

But I couldn't believe the latter was a motive.

Nobody kills somebody just to get land to pass on to family.

That night, there came a knock on the door. When I opened it, my jaw hit the floor. "Sheriff Perry. I'm surprised to see you."

His white Stetson was cocked on one side of his head. His normally flushed face was even more intense, almost matching his fiery red hair. "That surprises *me,* Boudreaux. I would have figured you'd know that I'd stop in sooner or later." He glanced to his left and right up and down the gallery. "May I come in?"

I opened the door wide. "Sure, come on in." I indicated Jack. "This is a friend, Jack Edney. Jack, Sheriff Perry."

Closing the door, I indicated a chair. "Make yourself comfortable, Sheriff. What brings you over here?"

He cut his eyes at Jack, then back at me.

"He's with me all the time, Sheriff. Sometimes I bounce ideas off Jack."

Jack smiled proudly.

The sheriff balked. "Then let's you and me go somewhere so we can talk."

The smile on Jack's face turned into a frown. "Never mind. I'd been planning on picking up a case of Budweiser anyway."

I winked at Jack. "Thanks."

After Jack left, I sat on the edge of the bed, facing the sheriff. "So, what did you want to talk about?"

He eyed me narrowly. In a gruff voice, he replied, "I always want to know when an outsider comes into my jurisdiction and starts asking questions that are none of his business."

Chapter Twenty-seven

I stiffened, then forced myself to relax. Glibly, I replied, "I don't understand what you're driving at, Sheriff."

A wry smile cracked his somber face. He pulled out a chair and sat. "Come on, Boudreaux. Don't play games. We're country out here, but not all of us are hicks. I know you've prowled around at Barton's and at the cemetery. I suspect you and the fat boy are the ones who dug up the spaceman's grave. On top of that, you been asking questions about Jim Bob Houston. Now, last I heard, Jim Bob disappeared about twenty years ago. No way can I see what Jim Bob had to do with the demise of Justin Chester." He leaned back in his chair and folded his arms across his chest. "So, tell me. What are you up to?"

I studied him for a moment. "I guess you could say that I'm just the curious sort, Sheriff."

He stared at me for several moments, trying to make up his mind about something. What, I had no idea, except I didn't figure he would attempt anything in here, since Jack was aware of his presence.

"I think you're lying." He paused. When he continued, his gruff words became accommodating. "Now, look. I'm not interested in creating any problems for you or your company with the state. From what I've heard around town, I figure you suspect something happened to Jim Bob Houston, and you're trying to find out what. Why, I don't know, but that's what I'm guessing."

I started to protest, but he held up a hand. "Hear me out. I never bought the business of Jim Bob's moving to Chicago, but I never could run him down. Every place I looked was a dead end. In the early nineties, maybe ninety-one, I lost the trail at a place run by some folks named Talley. Talked to some old woman who'd rented a room to a Jim Bob Houston, but he didn't recognize Jim Bob's picture." He paused and studied me. "Mind telling me what you're up to? Maybe I can help."

For several moments, I hesitated. Finally, I replied. "I wasn't certain about you. Like, why didn't you recognize Justin Chester's name when I first came to you? He'd been here five or six months."

His eyebrows furrowed in confusion, then rose in understanding. He chuckled. "Because I'd never heard the name or met him. Yeah, I saw a guy in ragged clothes riding a bicycle back and forth to school, but I never met him. His hair was short, not long like in the snapshot you showed me."

"Never heard his name?"

"If I had, I would have told you."

"But the principal, Georgiana Irvin. She said she asked you for a criminal background check on him."

He laughed. "That's because Lisa Simmons, my secretary, file clerk, and general all-around problem-solver does it for me. Georgiana asked Lisa. She's been with me since the beginning. We're a small community, Boudreaux. Hey, if someone wanted a background check, and I answered the phone, they'd ask for Lisa. You know what I mean? She takes care of half my business, and when she thinks I need to know something, she tells me."

His explanation made sense in a casual sort of way. Nodding slowly, I replied, "I can follow that, but what about Chester's death certificate?"

He frowned, puzzled. "What about it? George was in Fort Worth, so I filled it out. He looked at Chester and the truck when he got back and signed it. What's the problem?"

His candor surprised me, but then, I couldn't help wondering if it was candor or a sly skewing of the truth. "The injury was to the back of his head, not his forehead."

Perry studied me for a moment before shaking his head. "Yeah, that was strange, wasn't it? Chester had both hands at the top of the steering wheel. Best George and me could figure was, his head banged into them, then bounced back and hit the cab. The only spot on his forehead came from the class ring on his finger. Screwy, huh?"

I considered his explanation, remembering the dime-sized impression Tricia had mentioned. It made sense. Slowly, I nodded. "Yeah."

He leaned forward. "So, now that we have that cleared up, let's talk about Houston. How far have you gotten into running him down?"

I was at one of those spots in life that demanded a decision I didn't want to make. I had a couple of other questions, but

I didn't want to commit myself. Should I trust Perry or not? I had the queasy feeling that I was caught in a whirlpool and couldn't fight my way out. Then I thought of a third option. "Why don't you tell me what you know?"

He eyed me several moments, an amused gleam in his eyes. "Okay. One of us has got to start." He nodded to the ice chest on Jack's bed. "Any beer in there?"

"Should be. My friend gets panicky when he's down to his last six-pack." I pulled out a couple and tossed Perry one. We popped the tabs.

He took several long gulps and leaned back. "I think Houston is dead. I don't believe he ever went to Chicago." He went on to tell me what I already knew, about Houston and Ford's falling out, the land argument, the suit and judgment, and Houston's disappearing.

I remembered hearing the story, although with a few discrepancies. "Is Ford the kind to resort to violence?"

Perry arched a skeptical eyebrow. "Anyone, Mr. Boudreaux, given the right set of circumstances, can resort to violence."

I raised an eyebrow.

He continued. "Like I said, I showed Houston's picture to Mrs. Talley. He didn't recognize him." He leaned forward. "That's all I know. Now, what about you? Are you the one who dug up the grave? It wasn't spotted until yesterday after the snow melted. Couple of high school kids out rabbit hunting saw it and reported it."

I didn't know exactly where I was going with all this, but my choices were growing fewer and fewer. I decided to open up a little. "After Justin Chester came back here, he called and told me he had found what he was looking for. After his inheritance, he had the money to exhume the coffin. Of course, he would have gone through the legal process, which would have taken him some time, but I think that's what he had on his mind." I rose and stood at the window, looking out into the gathering darkness. I sipped my Budweiser and turned to face the sheriff. "He found the grave."

Perry's eyes narrowed skeptically.

I pulled the copies of Justin's papers from my briefcase and rolled them out on the table before him. "Here is a plat of the cemetery, and the spot he marked up here is where we found the grave. The other papers are notes, inventory, that sort of thing." I paused and chuckled. "By the way, those are copies. The originals are in my office safe in Austin." I glanced at the originals lying in plain sight in my briefcase. As soon as he left, I planned to get those papers where they would be safe.

Just in case.

Perry grinned up at me. "You're not one to take chances, huh?"

"Believe me, I've had more than my share of misfortune because I foolishly took an unnecessary chance."

Rolling his massive shoulders, Perry smoothed the plat of the cemetery with his large hands. He jabbed a meaty finger at the circle. "That's where you dug, huh?"

"It wasn't that easy, Sheriff. Barton told us to look for a metal rod below the surface of the grass. He and Justin had put it there."

Perry sneered. "Barton? But he was nothing but an old drunk always fighting the DTs."

"Maybe so, but he steered us to the right place." I hesitated, then pulled out the folder of snapshots and thumbed through to the ones in the grave. "Take a look." I handed them to Perry.

He studied them for several moments, his face concentrated in a frown. "What am I looking for?"

I pointed to the bones in the casket. "This casket is about three and a half feet long. These remains were cut in half to fit into the casket. Take a look at the femur, the left leg above the knee." I pointed it out. "See how it's bent? Newt Gibons told me that years ago, Jim Bob broke his leg. He took him to the hospital, but they didn't set it right. Left leg. He hobbled around on it."

Gus Perry nodded. "I don't remember which leg, but he did limp after that."

I leaned back. "There it is. And with your authority, we can get a DNA on the remains in the grave to positively identify them as Jim Bob Houston."

He looked up at me. "So what happened? How did he end up in that grave?"

For a moment, I hesitated. With information, a person has leverage, and I was giving it all away. Still, I was beginning to trust Perry. His explanation about not recognizing Justin's name made sense. He knew that Jim Bob had supposedly gone to Chicago and had tried to run him down. Otherwise, how would he have known the name of Homer Talley? His explanation of the death certificate made sense, however inappropriately handled.

He prodded me. "Well?"

I gathered the pictures and stuck them back into my briefcase.

"I suppose you have the negatives for those somewhere else, huh?"

"Yep. In my office safe in Austin." Which was another lie on my part.

He shrugged. "Fine with me. What else do you have?"

I studied him carefully. "I can tell you who I think is involved in Jim Bob's disappearance. I'm not sure why, but I think I know at least one, maybe two individuals."

Sheriff Perry downed the rest of his Budweiser and crushed the can in his hand, a feat of no consequence today when compared to the cans of yesteryear. "Who?"

Without hesitation, I replied. "Marvin Lewis!"

Chapter Twenty-eight

I don't know what reaction I expected from the sheriff, but his casual acceptance of my accusation surprised me, making me wonder if perhaps he had his own suspicions regarding Marvin Lewis. Calmly, he asked, "Mind telling me why?"

"As I understand events around here, Sara Ann Houston left Jim Bob around eighty-three or four. A love triangle. In eighty-six, Houston vanished and supposedly rented an apartment in Chicago. No one seems to know who the third member of that love triangle was." I stared at Perry for a response.

He rose from his chair and pulled another Budweiser from the ice chest. With a grin, he quipped, "Your buddy better get back with a fresh supply if this keeps up." He chugged several long swallows, then said, "There was a bunch of wild guesses about the other guy—that's all." His red face turned crimson. "I was even brought into it, not that Sara Ann wasn't a looker. She was, but I was just like the others around here. I couldn't believe it when word got out."

"Marvin Lewis was the third leg of that triangle," I announced simply.

A baffled frown contorted Sheriff Perry's face, but not for the reason I thought. He stammered. "W-What?"

"Sara, Jim Bob, and good old Marv. And for your information, I got it from the horse's mouth."

"Marvin told you?"

"Sara Ann."

He sat back in the chair, shaking his head and muttering a soft curse. "That I never would have believed. Why, Marv is twenty years or more older than her."

I couldn't resist wisecracking, "You've heard the old saying about snow on the roof, haven't you?"

Perry laughed. "Yeah. When you get to be my age, you hear a lot of those old stories. Unfortunately, some might be true, but most aren't."

We both laughed, probably to keep from crying.

"And, second," I added, "Nora Talley, the widow of the man you talked to in Chicago, identified Marvin Lewis as the man who rented the apartment in Jim Bob Houston's name."

The smile fled Perry's face. "You're kidding me."

Unsmiling, I shook my head slowly.

For several moments, he sat staring at the beer in his hand. Finally, he looked up. "You said maybe two. Who's the other one?"

"Buck Ford. He lied about seeing the pickup in the creek. From where he was, it's impossible to see down there. And according to Sara Ann, he and J. B. hated each other, especially after Houston won the judgment against Ford."

Perry blew through his lips. "Well, sure looks like—"

At that moment, Jack popped back in, halting in the doorway. "All right? Or do I need to get some more beer?"

I looked at Perry. He shrugged. "Come on in, Jack," I said. "Now, Sheriff, I think you were going to say something when Jack interrupted."

He eyed me narrowly. "You seem to have this pretty well figured out."

"Not really. I've got some ideas, but just as many questions."

He leaned forward. "Such as? Maybe I can fill some in."

"First, Houston's wife and Lewis had a thing going. She left, and Houston sold out to Lewis two or three years later. Why?" I paused, then added, "If my wife had an affair with some guy, he'd be the last one I'd want to deal with. How about you?"

He frowned, contemplating the question. He shook his head. "Money has a way of changing a guy's perspective. You know what I mean?"

"Yeah." I knew exactly what he meant. Money can buy just about anything, which is a chilling indictment of our society today.

"What about the contract? Was it legal?"

I rummaged through my briefcase and handed him a copy of the deed on record. "See for yourself. Here's the deed they filed back in eighty-six. Fully notarized and filed accordingly in the county clerk's Office."

He skimmed the document and shrugged. "Looks legal to me."

"It is."

With a shrug, he returned the contract. "Looks like money made Jim Bob forget what happened."

I continued. "Now, as far as Houston's disappearance, the only link is the fact that Lewis was the one who rented the apartment in Chicago. Everything else is a matter of conjecture, one person's word against another's. But, if you will authorize DNA testing on the remains in the grave, then we can find out if the remains are Houston's. If they are not, I'm full of bull, we're back to square one, and I'm waltzing on down to Austin."

He pushed himself to his feet. "You've given me a lot to think about. I don't know as I agree with you or not, but I'll sure look into a DNA test on those bones. You come up with something concrete we can use, let me know." He offered his hand.

I shook it, then added, "One more question before you go."

"Shoot."

"Harlan Barton saw two men, he didn't know who, bury Houston twenty years ago. He couldn't identify them. Why didn't he tell you about it?"

Perry pursed his lips. The wrinkles in his face folded like an accordion. "Probably because he knew I wouldn't believe him. Back in the seventies, he must have called me out to the cemetery a dozen times, each time swearing he had found the grave of the spaceman and wanted me to dig it up." He shrugged. "That's the best answer I got."

And it made sense in a screwy sort of way.

I stood on the gallery watching the sheriff drive from the parking lot. While I had revealed to him a great deal, I had also picked up a few choice pieces of information. I drew a deep breath and let it out slowly.

I just hoped I had not made a mistake in trusting him.

As usual, Jack was hungry, so we headed down to the restaurant. I had not eaten since breakfast, and I was hungry enough to tackle one of the restaurant's highly advertised sixteen-, thirty-two–, or forty-eight–ounce broiled rib eyes with sides of cream gravy, French fries, buttered rolls, and topped off with hot apple pie smothered in Blue Bell homemade vanilla ice cream.

I gained five pounds just reading the menu, but that's what I ordered, specifying, I might add, the sixteen-ounce steak. Jack, naturally, opted for the forty-eight.

Texas truck stop dining is a world of its own, filled with unimaginable and delectable delights that would never occur to the average man. T-bones, sirloins, ribs, chops, chicken, and even the hamburgers were all man-sized, daring a diner to put it all down and walk out without staggering.

I had learned the hard way, but Jack was still trying to climb that hill. His rib eye filled one platter, his fries another, and they were accompanied by a bowl of steaming white cream gravy and a platter of yeasty rolls soaked with butter.

It was a glutton's dream.

I could have eaten on it for a week and then had some left over.

Halfway through our meal, Mabel Hooker walked in with a large man bundled into a brown nylon parka and wearing a western hat. She spotted us and waved. I returned the gesture, and they made their way over to us.

She had to be the smilingest woman I've ever known. Freezing cold outside, and she was smiling. Burning hot, and she was smiling. Raining frogs, and she was smiling. She never quit. "Hi, boys. Heard about the accident. Glad you're okay."

"Not as much as we are." I glanced at the man beside her. He was a head taller than Mabel and probably ten years older. His eyes were the clearest light blue I had ever seen, somehow reminding me of the eyes of all of those western plainsman I had read about as a kid.

She introduced us. "This is Gabe, my husband. Gabe, this is Tony and Jack, the city boys from Austin I told you about."

Gabe grinned, revealing a set of teeth with half a dozen gaps in them. "Howdy, boys."

"By the way, Mabel, I've been wondering. Harlan Barton. When's his funeral?"

"Tomorrow. The Christian church. Next door to the feed store right across the highway from Cemetery Road."

For a moment, I hesitated, unsure how to approach the subject. "I'd like to contribute to any expenses, but I don't want to create any problems. I know Harlan wasn't all that well off."

She grinned. "It's taken care of. Old Buck Ford, he's paying for it all."

At first, the announcement surprised me, then I remembered seeing Barton climb into the pickup with Ford. "That's a nice gesture on his part," I replied.

Gabe swept a big gnarled hand in front of his face as if to say "no gesture at all." "Buck and Harlan went way back, Boudreaux. Harlan's daddy gave Buck his first job. Buck never forgot that. So, after Harlan fell on bad times, old Buck, despite all his sins—" He paused to laugh. "He always looked after Harlan." He looked down at his wife with an expression of love I've seldom seen and hugged her to him. "That's how we are out here."

Mabel snorted and jerked away. A crooked grin on her face, she muttered gruffly, "You talk too much, Gabe. Let's eat. See you boys later."

If I had not been convinced of Buck Ford's involvement, Mabel Hooker had handed me the final piece.

If Buck Ford cared so much for Harlan Barton, then he had to know that Barton and Justin Chester were working together. From the little time I had spent with Barton, he was anything but an unforthcoming individual. On the contrary, he was as garrulous as one of my *grandpère's* old sows when someone grabbed one of her piglets.

I couldn't help wondering if Barton had informed Buck Ford of what he and Justin were doing. In fact, from what I had just learned, I would have been willing to bet that Harlan Barton had told Buck Ford everything they were up to.

In all probability, Harlan told Ford he and Justin had discovered the location of the spaceman's grave. That's when Ford decided he and Lewis had no choice but to off Justin Chester.

A tiny frown knit my brow. Something puzzled me. If Ford had killed Justin, why did he report the "accident"? Why not let someone else find the body? Unless he was just trying to be clever.

Suddenly I wasn't hungry. I pushed back from the table. "Go ahead and finish up, Jack. I'm going on up to the room. I've got some work to do. Sign the check for me."

He looked at me oddly for a moment, then shrugged. His answer was another forkful of ketchup-covered rib eye steak popped into his mouth.

Outside, I changed my mind and headed for my pickup. I wanted to talk to Mr. Buck Ford.

Chapter Twenty-nine

I found Buck Ford in his barn beneath one of the massive conveyors belts that carried feed to the cattle in his feedlots. He looked up from under the clattering belt of rollers when I approached, a smear of grease across his forehead. He frowned; then a gleam of recognition lit his eyes. "Boudreaux, ain't it?"

"Yeah."

He crawled out from under the conveyor and, despite his huge belly, climbed agilely to his feet. Monkey wrench in hand, he waved to his men. "Keep at it, boys. I got three hundred head to fatten up before I send them out in the morning. The more money lining my pockets, the more in yours, ain't that right?"

"You bet, Buck," they chorused, turning back to repairing the conveyor.

Pointing the monkey wrench at me, he said, "So, Mr. Boudreaux. What can I do for you?"

"First, I heard you were taking care of Harlan Barton's funeral. I want you to know, that's a mighty decent thing. I knew him only a short time, and if I wouldn't offend you, I'd be grateful to contribute to the expenses."

Perplexed, he eyed me for a few moments. "Now, why would you want to do that?"

"Probably, Buck, for the same reason you're doing it. I liked the old man."

Buck snorted. "He was loony."

"Maybe so, but being nuts doesn't keep someone from being likeable."

Ford laughed. "You're right, Boudreaux. Mighty right. Forget the money. I appreciate it. Besides, my accountant will figure some way to write it off. Now, anything else I can do for you?"

"Harlan ever tell you what he and Chester were up to?"

He raised a skeptical eyebrow. "That spaceman nonsense? No. After Chester come back to town, I didn't see much of old Harlan. He was spending all his time with Chester." He drew a deep breath. "Anything else?"

I eyed the monkey wrench in his hand. For a moment, I wavered, then mustered the courage and said, "I don't understand your version of spotting Justin Chester's pickup in the creek. When I went to the bridge, the vegetation along the east bank blocked any sight of the pickup."

He studied me a moment, obviously puzzled. "Nobody can see anything in that part of the creek from the bridge."

"You did. You said you did. I heard you tell your men that you spotted it."

I expected some sort of angry, defensive response, but he simply stared at me with a perplexed expression. "I don't understand. I was driving onto the bridge when the pickup bounced off the tree, then wobbled the few yards to the bank and fell in." He held out his hands, the monkey wrench still grasped in one. "That's it. That's all I saw. It was dark, so dark I almost didn't see it. I had to have a flashlight to recognize Chester. Now, if I said anything to make you think otherwise, then I apologize. But that's how it was. I didn't see the pickup go through the fence, but I did see it bounce off the tree and fall into the creek." He paused, his frown growing deeper. "What are you driving at, Boudreaux? I thought you were here to pick up Chester's gear and skedaddle on back to Austin."

I glanced around the barn. His men were busy on the conveyor. "I've talked to Sheriff Perry about my suspicions. He knows I'm asking these questions."

His cheeks were beginning to grow red. "What suspicions?"

"That Justin Chester's death was somehow linked to that of Jim Bob Houston."

Either Buck was a consummate actor, or he was genuinely perplexed. "What do you mean about Houston's death? Jim Bob moved to Chicago. A couple of years later he dropped out of sight. No one ever heard from him again."

Shaking my head slowly, I gave him a wry grin. "He never reached Chicago. Someone rented an apartment under his name. Kept him 'alive' for two or three years, then let him vanish."

He stared at me in disbelief, which then turned to belligerence. "You think I had something to do with it?" he demanded.

"No. Otherwise, the landlady would have identified you.

But there's a couple of questions that puzzle me. You didn't like him, did you?" I asked abruptly.

Unperturbed, he grunted. "Hated his guts, and he hated mine."

"Why?"

He stared at me for a moment, then rolled his shoulders. "Family problems back two or three generations. And don't ask what they were, because I don't know. I grew up despising Jim Bob Houston, and he did the same with me. And then a lawsuit."

"A hundred thousand, I heard. Makes for a nice motive."

A crooked grin played over his lips. "Sure would if he hadn't been paid off." He paused. "But I ain't lying when I said we hated each other. I don't know what happened to him, and I don't care. I'm just glad he's gone."

I shook my head in wonder. "Kinda surprising admission for such a tight community, huh?"

With a snort, he replied, "Nothing tight about Elysian Hills—I guarantee you that."

"What do you think happened to Jim Bob?"

He pounded the monkey wrench into the palm of his hand with a loud slap. "I don't know, and I don't care. All I know is, it took me three years to pay off the lawsuit that no-account filed on me."

I had him talking, so I popped him another question. "Did anyone around here have reason to kill him?"

He considered for a moment. "No. No one hated him like me, and I certainly didn't kill him. That is, if he is dead." He eyed me narrowly.

"What about his ex-wife?"

"Sara Ann? No. Decent woman." When he saw me raise an eyebrow, he chuckled. "Hey, everyone is entitled to a couple of mistakes. Her first was marrying the jerk. The second was when she played around on him."

"With whom? Someone in Elysian Hills?"

He started to shake his head, then mumbled, "No one knows. There was a little talk about her and Marv, but I didn't put no stock in it. Marv is twenty years older than her." He paused and eyed me warily. "So what does all this have to do with that Chester dude?"

I studied him for a moment. With a terse shake of my head, I lied. "I don't know. Probably nothing."

Sitting in my pickup, I studied the well-lit metal barn. I couldn't see that Buck Ford had had motive enough to murder Jim Bob. Of course, family feuds can reignite with one wrong word. According to Barton, he saw two people digging up the grave. Marv Lewis was probably one of them. Ford could have been the other. And, I told myself, he might not have been.

I pulled up to the stop sign on the top of the hill at the junction of the graveled drive and FM 1287. As far as I could see to the west was absolute darkness with two or three pinholes of light. Back to the east, a few security lights illuminated Elysian Hills, casting globes of silver on the ground.

I pulled onto the highway and headed for the motel. After I passed the intersection of Cemetery Road and the highway, I glanced into my rearview mirror. Headlights popped on, and the glow of a security light revealed a small white car speeding over the hill toward Woodbine.

Taggart!

I wheeled about, but when I topped the hill, the head-lights had vanished.

The only lights around were those at Buck Ford's barn.

Chapter Thirty

Jack was snoring away when I reached our room.

Turning on the lamp over the desk, I opened my brief-case to pull out my notes. An envelope fell out of one of the folders in the top of the case. I picked it up. It was my most recent Target bill for odds and ends for my apartment. I glanced at my address on Payton-Gin Road, Austin, Texas, 76756-6720. "Got to pay that as soon as I get back," I muttered, sliding the bill back into the folder.

I laid out all my notes and started back over them.

I had a gut feeling that Lewis was directly involved, but I couldn't come up with a motive. He had no reason to kill Jim Bob. Sara Houston had been gone two or three years. If the two had conspired, they wouldn't have waited so long to murder the man.

Had the situation been reversed, if Jim Bob had been fool-ing around with Marv's wife, I would have figured that was more than motive enough. But not the other way around.

Still, Nora Talley had identified him. That told me that, somehow, he had played a major role in Houston's disappearance.

Thirty minutes later, I shook my head and leaned back in my chair wearily.

The human mind is strange and mysterious. I don't know if it's true that we only utilize about ten percent of its capacity (and I probably use even less), but I do know that for me it is difficult at times to make that sucker go where I want it to.

Motive was what I sought. What could have prompted Marv Lewis to kill Jim Bob Houston? I could find nothing. Maybe I was looking in the wrong place or at the wrong person. I was still convinced that whoever murdered Houston had also killed Justin. The motive for Chester's death was simple. The killer didn't want Houston's body discovered.

At least I had Sheriff Perry on my side.

At breakfast, I got my first shock of the morning when a grim-looking Buck Ford strode in and made straight for our booth, brushing ice off the shoulders of his wool mackinaw.

He stopped and looked down. "Morning, boys. Mind if I join you?"

I started to scoot over, but he reached around and pulled a chair up to the end of the table. I introduced him to Jack. "You're out early."

His face remained grim. He glanced at Jack, then cut his eyes back to me.

I nodded. "He knows everything."

With a grunt, Ford rested his elbows on the table and stared straight into my eyes. "I got it from a good source. Watch your back. Whatever you're nosing into, someone don't like it." He hastened to add, "I don't know any more than that. All I was told last night was to warn you that someone don't like your snooping around, and they reckon on stopping you."

Leaning back, I eyed him narrowly. "This source. Who is it?"

He pursed his lips. "He's my cousin. That's all I'll tell you, but he overheard talk that you were getting too close, and something needed to be done about you."

I stared after Ford as he left the restaurant, wondering just which one of the townsfolk was his cousin. If Elysian Hills was like most small communities, it could be anyone.

Jack glanced up at me uneasily. "You think he was serious, Tony?"

I was convinced then that Ford had no part in either murder. Slowly I nodded. "As cancer."

As we started up the stairs to our room, I suddenly froze, remembering the zip code on my Target bill. Prior to the fifties, most communication was by mail. Mom, as did her mother, saved every letter from family members. I remembered looking at the faded envelopes, curious, and asking why zip codes were on our envelopes today and not on the old ones. Mom had smiled. "We didn't have them then, son."

An idea struck me. I bounded up the stairs.

Behind me, Jack was yelling, "What's wrong, Tony? What's wrong?"

In our room, I booted up the computer and pulled up zip

codes on a search engine. My heart thudded in my chest. The first use of the five-digit zip code was in 1963. The nine-digit came in 1986.

I pulled out the deed I had copied up in Montague County at the courthouse.

There, at the bottom of the deed contract, was the notarized statement of Pearl Ragsdale, P.O. Box 749, Elysian Hills, Texas, 76251-4963 verifying the legality of the signatures. What jumped out at me was the date, November 23, 1985, two months before the nine-digit zip code went into effect.

The document was forged!

I must have exploded in a string of gleeful cursing, for Jack hurried over to me. "What's wrong, Tony? Huh? What is it?"

I pointed to the screen. "We've got him nailed, Jack. Marvin Lewis." I tapped my middle finger on the sales document. "This is a forgery."

He frowned at me.

I was so excited, I was shaking. "All right. Let me explain what took place. For whatever reason, Marvin Lewis killed Jim Bob Houston in 1986. That's when Houston disappeared. I'm going to guess in March, because that's when the deed was filed. Lewis buried him in the empty spaceman's grave, had the contract drawn up, notarized, and filed, rented a room in Chicago under Houston's name, and put money in the bank in Houston's name. Two years later, he let Houston vanish. Where Pearl Ragsdale made her mistake notarizing the document was using the nine-digit zip code that had gone into effect two months earlier."

Jack frowned. "I don't follow you."

I drew a deep breath. "All right. Look, in January of eighty-six, a nine-digit zip code went into effect. Okay? Using it had become habit for the notary, Pearl Ragsdale. So much of a habit, in fact, that when she backdated the sales contract to November of the previous year, she forgot to use only the five-digit zip in effect at that time. Now do you follow me?"

Jack's brow knit. "I'm no genius, but couldn't someone get into a bunch of trouble backdating documents like that?"

I laughed. I don't know if it was at his remark, or I was so giddy over my discovery. "No idea. Maybe."

"Then why do it?"

"Think about it," I replied, looking at the note card I had made on Pearl Ragsdale. "What's she got to lose? She's dying. Her forty-year-old son has to have special care to survive. She lived just down the road from Lewis. He knew her problems. He knew she had to have money, so he told her that if she would alter the dates, he would take care of her son, Ollie, after her death by placing him in St. Christopher's in Fort Worth. She has nothing to lose and everything to gain. And with the contract, Lewis tied up Houston's disappearance in a neat little package. You'll pardon me for saying so, it was a match made in heaven."

Jack nodded and muttered, "Or hell."

Turning back to my notes, I jotted down my information, after which I pulled up the St. Christopher's Web site. Tuition began at six hundred a month, probably a third that sum back in the eighties. On impulse, I called St. Christopher's. Under the pretext of searching for heirs to mineral rights, I learned that Oliver Ragsdale, who had entered school in June 1986, was deceased. Date, November 2, 1996, at age fifty-two.

I studied the document, trying to sort my thoughts into a logical chronology. If it were filed in March 1986, chances were, that was when Houston was killed—the same month the apartment was rented from Homer and Nora Talley in Evanston. Ragsdale notarized the document that month, backdating it to November of 1985. Three months after notarizing it, she passed away, and Marvin Lewis saw to it that little Ollie was placed at St. Christopher's.

Elated, I picked up the phone to call Sheriff Perry, but at the last moment I hesitated when my glance fell onto one of my note cards. I picked it up. It was about one of the first conversations I had had with Marvin Lewis. At the time of Justin's death, claimed Lewis, he was at his brother's in Gainesville, northeast of Elysian Hills.

On impulse, I drew up the white pages online, and, to my dismay, there were over thirty Lewises in Gainesville. I went back to my note cards and with a sigh of relief found the brother's name, Benjamin.

There were no Benjamins, but there were three B. Lewises. On the second call, I got the right one. I told him I was Joe Ragsdale, an old friend of Marvin's. "I tried him at home, and there was no answer. Then I remembered at the end of last month, he was out of town. Someone said he might have gone to your place for a visit. I thought he might be there now, with the holidays coming up."

"Sorry, Mr. Ragsdale. He isn't here. I haven't seen my brother since last Christmas. It's shame, you know. Families aren't close like they used to be."

"I know, Mr. Lewis. Thanks anyway. Sorry to bother you."

With a grin as wide as the Colorado River, I punched off my cell and looked at Jack. "I think we got something."

Before Jack could ask, I continued. "Lewis told me he was visiting his brother the day Justin died. He lied. Now, why would he lie?"

"Simple. Because he did it."

I dialed the sheriff's number, but he was out.

I grabbed my jacket. "Let's go."

After the cut brake lines, I made a routine habit of pumping the brakes hard every time I climbed behind the wheel. It's a mighty uneasy feeling flying down the road at fifty or sixty miles an hour and slamming on the brakes only to have them go to the floor.

The weather had turned miserable; the low gray clouds dropped a steady drizzle of ice. It was the kind of day that called for a warm fire and a smooth drink.

Halfway to Elysian Hills, I spotted Perry's cruiser coming toward us. When he saw my Silverado, he pulled off the shoulder and climbed out. I parked on the shoulder across the road from him.

Bundled in a heavy, fur-collared nylon jacket, he hurried across the road, slapping his arms to keep the blood flowing.

I rolled the window down. "I tried to call you."

Turning his shoulder into the falling drizzle, he shouted, "Yeah? What about?"

"I have proof that the deed for Houston's land was a forgery. And I can prove that Lewis was not at his brother's like he claimed when Justin Chester was killed. It looks like Lewis killed Chester to keep him from digging up the spaceman's grave, where, twenty years earlier, he'd buried Jim Bob Houston."

"What about Buck Ford?"

I shrugged. "I was wrong."

Perry studied me for a moment. "All right. How do you figure Marv managed all that?"

Suddenly, my brain started clicking. "He must have killed Justin during the day, maybe up at his house, or in Justin's room. Struck him on the back of his head. Then, after dark, he drove him out to the creek and sent the pickup toward the water, but it hit the tree and bounced off." I remembered the stench of gasoline in the pickup. "He probably figured it would crash and burn, but it didn't. That's when Buck spotted it."

The sheriff eyed me suspiciously. "So why didn't Buck spot Marv?"

I grimaced, then remembered the car tracks leading behind the patch of shinnery. The words rushed from my lips. "Like Buck said, it was dark. Lewis had parked his car behind the shinnery patch. He waited back there until Buck left to notify you, then headed in the other direction."

Pursing his lips, the sheriff replied, "Okay. Tell me. How did Marv manage to get his car and the pickup out there if he was the only one driving?"

His question stumped me. I had eliminated Ford and Perry. Who was left? "I don't know. But he had help."

"Who?"

I blew out through my lips. "I told you. I don't know. Someone here in Elysian Hills. You know these people better than I do."

Perry blinked and shook his head slowly. "You think that's the way it was, huh?"

"Makes sense, through I could be wrong. However, I am certain about the deed and Lewis' brother."

"Well, you'd better be, because that Talley woman in Chicago had a heart attack last night. She died this morning. That's what I was coming to tell you."

I groaned.

He looked up at the weather. "Look. This stuff's going to get worse. Get on back to the motel. I'll get in touch with you this afternoon, and we'll decide where to go from here."

I studied him for a moment. "I want to clean up a couple of things in town. Won't take long. We'll be at the motel when you call."

For a moment, his eyes flashed, then he nodded. "All right, but take care on these roads. They'll start icing over directly. You've already been through one fence." He chuckled. "Don't try for two.

Chapter Thirty-one

Icicles dangled from the eaves of Sam Fuqua's convenience store. The parking lot was empty. We jumped out of the pickup and scurried into the warmth of the small business.

Sam greeted us with a broad smile and a gesture at the coffeepot.

Pouring a mug of his own, he joined us in front of the space heater. "Terrible day," he muttered with a shiver. "Never no business on days like this. Once I started to close early on one of these days, but a man, he came in. He run out of gas down the road. So, I tell myself never to close early. You never can tell when someone might come in."

"Never can tell," I replied.

"So, what brings you out on such a day as this one?"

"Oh, a couple of questions about Jim Bob Houston. You grew up with him. What kind of man was he?"

The small man frowned at me. "Why you ask?"

"No reason. Just curious. I've heard so much about him, I just wondered what he was like."

Sam shrugged. "He was a good man. He was our mayor when he was young, right out of high school. Then he married, and the marriage was good. At least, I thought it was. My wife, she say different, but all that she hear was gossip. Then Sara Ann leave, and Jim Bob, he start drinking heavy. Once, when he was drunk, he jumped Sheriff Perry, saying he was the one that caused Sara Ann to leave."

"The sheriff?"

"Yes, but Jim Bob, he was drunk." He paused and sipped his coffee. "He was one of those mean drunks. Not the happy kind that finds a corner and goes to sleep. He went looking for trouble. He caused trouble with many around here. The truth is, while we was all surprised to see him leave, we were glad inside, you know? No more drunk trouble."

"How'd the sheriff react?"

Sam shrugged. "After Jim Bob leave, I never heard him say a bad word about the man."

On the way back to the motel, Jack asked, "What was that all about?"

I turned my ideas over in my head, then bounced them off Jack. "Look, if Lewis was involved, he had to have a reason. He has everything any man could want—money, land, family. What reason would he have to kill Houston?"

Jack shrugged. "Beats me."

"Beats me too." A rabbit dashed across the road in front of us. I swerved, and the Silverado's back end broke loose, sending us fishtailing down the icy road. Sweat popped out on my forehead, and my fingers dug into the steering wheel. After a short distance, I managed to straighten the pickup.

Jack whistled. "Whew! That was close. One accident is enough."

His remark triggered a response in my brain. "Maybe that's what it was, Jack, an accident."

"Huh? What?"

"Houston's death. Sam says Houston did a lot of drinking after his wife left. He confronted Sheriff Perry. What if he confronted Marvin Lewis and, in the struggle, Houston was accidentally killed?"

With a shrug, Jack grunted. "So, why didn't he report it to the sheriff as an accident?"

All I could do was shake my head.

Back at the motel, we waited impatiently for Sheriff Perry. I was eager to get the skeletal remains to a lab for the DNA analysis. A positive identification would set the judicial process into motion. Slow motion, but motion nevertheless, and the inexorable movement of the process usually ended in justice.

The telephone broke the silence.

It was Tricia Chester. Two questions were on her mind.

The first: "Had Justin mentioned anything about being a member of the Masonic Lodge?"

"Not to me, Tricia. Why?"

"Well, the junkman who has Justin's pickup sent your office the setting of a Masonic ring someone found in Justin's pickup. Blue with the Masonic seal on it. Mr. Blevins sent it out to us. If we'd known he was a Mason, we could have had Masonic rites."

"Was he wearing a ring?"

"Only one. His high school graduation ring."

I grimaced. "I'm sorry. He never mentioned it."

She cleared her throat. "And, not that I mind, but Frank and Vanessa are wondering when you'll be back. They think everything should have been taken care of by now."

I was torn between telling her the truth or making up a story.

At that moment, there came a knock on the door. Jack opened it. Sheriff Perry stepped inside, brushing a light dusting of snow from his shoulders.

I waved to the sheriff. "Look, Tricia. Something just came up. Something important. I'll call you back when it's over." Without giving her time to respond, I hung up. "Hello, Sheriff."

With a curt nod, he hooked a thumb over his shoulder. "Boudreaux. Edney. Get your stuff, and let's go."

"Go? Where?"

"Why, to see Marvin Lewis and hear what he has to say about all this. After all, every dog has his day in court, right?"

The hair on the back of my neck bristled at his suggestion. "You sure? Now?"

He nodded emphatically. "Sure. I want to get this settled. You have some strong evidence. I want to see how he responds. Look at him. He's a ninety-year-old man. What can he do?"

"If you say so." I grabbed my coat. "You going, Jack?"

He shook his head. "Too cold out there."

Sheriff Perry laughed. "Come on. You'll enjoy the drive. You'll go nuts staying in the motel all the time. Besides, tonight's when Marv whips up his homemade chili. You've never eaten chili until you take a bite of Marv's. Might as well kill two birds with one stone."

"But, won't he wonder what Jack and I are doing there?"

"Look. This is a weekly thing with Marv. Sometimes I show up by myself; sometimes I invite someone else. He won't think a thing about it. While we're sitting around the table shooting the bull, you can hit him with what you have. Catch him off guard—know what I mean?"

I arched a skeptical eyebrow. "If you say so."

Downstairs, I started toward the pickup, but Sheriff Perry stopped me. "We can all go in the cruiser. I'll run you back here afterward. That'll give us a chance to talk about Marv's answers."

I shrugged. "Fine with me."

Marvin Lewis opened the door wearing a broad grin. "Howdy, Sheriff. I was expecting you on chili night. I see you brought company."

"Yep. Boudreaux and Mr. Edney wanted to sample that homemade chili of yours."

Lewis chuckled. "You boys are more than welcome. Come right on in. Take a seat at the kitchen table. I'll dish up the chili. I got plenty."

Puzzled, I glanced at Perry. He grinned at me.

I shrugged. It was a weird feeling. I'd never taken part in a criminal interview at a kitchen table eating chili and drinking beer. But then, I'd never lived in Elysian Hills either.

Wearing his trademark grin, the older man slid steaming bowls of chili onto the table along with a couple of bottles of ketchup and a platter of crackers. The beer was ice cold.

Perry banged the bottom of the ketchup bottle with the heel of one hand, popping three or four dollops onto his chili, after which he crumbled crackers over it and mixed them in thoroughly.

I remarked, "I thought only us country people in Louisiana ate our chili like that."

We both laughed.

Around a mouthful of chili. Perry said, "Reason we come over, Marv, is that Boudreaux here has turned up some evidence he thinks points to your being involved in Jim Bob's disappearance back in eighty-six."

To say I was surprised at just how abruptly the sheriff laid out my accusation was an understatement of the same magnitude as saying the Grand Canyon was nothing more than a drainage ditch.

Marv paused with a heaping spoonful of chili at his lips. With a grin, he said, "Oh? And what might that be, Mr. Boudreaux?"

His self-assurance confused me. He was treating the accusation as a lark. I glanced at Jack, who for once wasn't feeding his face. He was watching the two of us. I cleared my throat and said, "First, there's the title deed on the six sections of land. It was dated November 1985, but the notary used a nine-digit zip code. Nine-digit zips did not come into use until the next year, which tells me the document was backdated—in other words, forged."

He looked at me, confused. "Of course, I don't know how dear Pearl made a mistake like that, but I had nothing to do with it. Maybe she was hurting bad from the cancer, poor soul. I know she would never have done it intentionally." He looked at me with the innocence of a child.

"What about last November 28?"

"You mean when Justin had his accident?"

"It was no accident. You said you were visiting your brother in Gainesville, but he hasn't seen you in over a year."

He chuckled and took another bite of chili. "Benjamin's starting to lose it, Mr. Boudreaux. Sometimes he'll put on one sock and forget the other." He shook his white mane of hair. "Poor man."

I was growing frustrated with his insouciance. "All right, Nora Talley identified you as the one who rented the apartment in Chicago under the name Jim Bob Houston."

Leaning back, he frowned. "Oh." He paused, wrinkling his brow in concentration. "Isn't that the poor lady who had the heart attack?"

I cut my eyes sharply at Sheriff Perry. A faint sneer curled his lips.

I looked back at Marvin Lewis. He wore a patient but cold smile on his face. My gaze dropped to his hand, and I spotted a Masonic ring on his right ring finger. It was missing a setting.

Suddenly, like the proverbial bolt of lightning, it hit me. What a dummy I'd been. I was so absorbed in nailing Marre Lewis that I overlooked Buck Perry's lies. The Sheriff had fed me that story about showing a snapshot to Homer Talley in '90 or '91. He couldn't have. According to Talley's wife, Nora, Homer had died three years earlier in 1988.

The ominous click of a revolver hammer's being cocked froze me. Slowly, I turned to stare into the muzzle of a .38 with a four-inch barrel. Now, .38s might not be an elephant killer like the .357 or .44 magnum, but I can assure you, that tiny black hole in the muzzle of the smaller weapon is every bit as frightening when it is only two inches from your forehead.

Jack stared at me in confusion as I stammered to the sheriff, "You—You're part of it. Houston and Justin."

The cruel smile splitting his face was the only answer I needed.

Jack sat transfixed, chili dripping from the spoon halfway to his lips. For once, he'd lost his appetite. He was trying to speak, but nothing came out.

"You were the two that old man Barton saw digging the grave for Houston twenty years ago."

As if he were at a formal dinner, Marvin Lewis folded his napkin and laid it by his unfinished bowl of chili. "I told you someone was out there that night, Gus."

Perry nodded. "Yep. You did, Marv. Good idea you had about my going to see these two last night. Worked like a charm." He pushed himself back from the table and stared down at me. "I'd let you finish your meal, but I figure you've probably lost your appetite," he said with a sneer. He gestured with the muzzle of the .38. "Stand up. Put your hands behind your head."

In the heroic tradition of movie heroes, I hurled the bowl of chili and leaped from my chair at Perry. He anticipated my move and sidestepped. In the next second, he whacked me alongside my head, and I crumpled to the floor.

Chapter Thirty-two

I awakened as we bounced over a rough road. Outside, the snow and ice rat-a-tat-tatted against the sheriff's cruiser. Dashboard lights cast a dim glow through the steel mesh separating the front and back seats. My head throbbed.

Jack was at my side, jostling me with his shoulder. He whispered urgently, "Tony, wake up. You hear me? Wake up!"

Through the foggy mist in my head, I heard Perry laugh. "Waking up won't do him no good."

I managed to sit erect. I twisted at my bonds, but the plastic band cut into my wrists. I looked out the window. I saw nothing but absolute darkness except for the eerie reflection of the dash lights on the window. It was the kind of night a person could be murdered and buried and never found, especially out here in such desolate country.

We slowed and turned right. The lights struck Harlan Barton's dilapidated house. Perry stopped in back. The headlights illuminated the ramshackle barn. They pulled us out and looped ropes about our necks. Both Perry and Marvin Lewis carried handguns.

The bitter ice and snow struck our bare skin, chilling us to the marrow of our bones. Perry shoved us toward the barn. "Move."

We staggered forward. I blinked my eyes and shook my head, trying to clear the cobwebs. We couldn't make a break because of the ropes garroting our necks. My hands were bound behind my back, but, thanks to Jack's enormous girth, his hands were bound in front.

"Head for the barn."

The icy wind howled around us, nipping at our cheeks.

That's when I remembered the seed room. I glanced around, searching for a means of escape.

Perry jerked the rope on my neck, choking me. "Stop trying to figure out anything, Boudreaux. If you're a good Catholic, now's the time to be saying your Hail Mary's or whatever you say."

I gasped out, "Just tell me. Why Houston? I know Chester, but why Houston?"

Perry barked, "Don't tell him nothing, Marv. Nothing."

"What are they going to do? In ten minutes, they'll be nothing but smoke and ashes. They can't do a thing to us." He paused, then continued. "I'll tell you, Boudreaux. An accident. Just a stupid accident, but I was a state representative, and any scandal would have ruined me and Elysian Hills."

"Yeah," Perry put in. "The state had kept mineral rights to our area. Marv was within two votes in the state senate of getting the rights assigned to us like they should have been all along."

I listened incredulously. "You mean, you killed a man for oil and gas?"

Perry sneered. "Marv told you it was an accident. Besides, Jim Bob wasn't much of a man at the last."

"That's right," Marv offered. "He knew his wife and me had been fooling around. He got drunk one night and came over when Gus was there. Jim Bob jumped me. Gus yanked him off and threw him down. He hit his head on the fireplace hearth." He shivered. "Let's hurry up, Gus. It's getting colder. But that's all it was, an accident. And we weren't about to see where we had grown up, our parents had grown up, become nothing but a ghost town just because of a stupid accident of a drunk—not when all that money was out there waiting for us."

I laughed, which was a mistake. And I retorted, which turned out to be a bigger mistake, "Ghost town? What do you think this dump is now, downtown Dallas?"

The next thing I knew, the cold muzzle of a revolver slammed into the back of my head, knocking me to the ground. "That'll stop the wisecracks," Perry growled.

Rough hands jerked me up and shoved me toward the barn. "Get in there," Lewis snarled, shoving me forward.

I felt warm blood running down the back of my head. I couldn't think, but somewhere deep in the recesses of my brain, I remembered my pocketknife. If they were planning what I thought, to lock us in the seed room and burn the barn around us, we could use the pocketknife to free our hands. Then we could worry about escaping.

We stumbled into the barn, and they shoved us into the seed room. I stumbled to the floor and lay motionless, trying to still the pounding and swirling sensations in my skull. I felt the rough weave of empty burlap feed sacks pressing against my cheek.

Lewis spoke up. "You think we should leave them tied? What if the plastic ties don't burn?"

Perry sneered. "Don't worry. I'll be the first one out here. I'll make sure there's nothing for George to find."

"Just be sure. Sometimes old George takes that justice of the peace job too serious."

"I'll handle George like I did with Chester."

The door creaked shut.

I started to fumble for my knife, and then I heard Perry say, "Hold it."

Moments later, rough hands rolled me over and emptied my pockets. He chuckled. "I figured Boudreaux to carry a knife. All those farm boys do."

The door slammed shut.

Jack's voice quavered. "Tony, Tony! You awake?"

"Yeah," I muttered, struggling to sit up. I yanked at the plastic tie about my wrists, but there was no give, and Jack's fingers were too fat to depress the tiny tab in the clasp.

Moments later, the first wisps of acrid smoke seeped through the minute cracks in the seed bin. I scooted across the room and lay on my back so I could kick on the door. I remembered the heavy lock and the drop bar across the door. I didn't know if we could kick it down or not, but we had no other choice. "Get over here and help," I commanded Jack. "Maybe together, we can break this thing down."

We kicked at the door for several minutes as the smoke grew thicker, and then the faint crackling of fire reached us.

Suddenly, Jack exclaimed, "Tony! My nail clippers! You think they'll work? Huh, do you?"

Nail clippers! I closed my eyes. What did we have to lose? "Let's give it a try."

Jack grunted and groaned as he tried to reach into his pocket with both hands. "I can't do it, Tony. I can't get my arms around my belly."

Any other time, I would have laughed, but somehow, in that situation, I couldn't see the humor. I turned on my side. "All right. Scoot over to me. Find my hands and put your pocket next to them."

I blinked against the stinging smoke. Tears welled in my eyes and ran down my cheeks, and the acrid smoke was beginning to burn my lungs. The crackling of flames grew louder. I felt his trousers. My fingers searched for the pocket. "Okay, I've got your pocket. Now, let me see if I can get my hands down it."

"Hurry, hurry!"

After several futile efforts, I muttered a curse. "I can't get my hands down your pocket."

"Then turn it inside out," he exclaimed.

Inside out! Why hadn't I thought of that? I almost laughed at the irony of my situation. Here I'd just discovered my old pal was a genius, and I'd never live to enjoy his company.

Moments later, I passed the clippers to Jack, and he got busy nipping away at the plastic tie about my wrists.

The smoke grew thicker, the flames grew louder, and then we felt the heat.

Jack gasped. "Tony!"

"Keep trying, Jack. You're our only chance." I don't know if I believed that or not. Even if we freed ourselves, we still had to find some way to open the door before the smoke suffocated us.

From outside came the snapping of timber as joists began to fall.

Suddenly, my hands fell free.

With a crazy laugh, I rolled over. "You did it, Jack, you did it. Now give me your hands." Fumbling in the dark, I found the tab on the clamp and depressed it, permitting the plastic tie to slide free.

Coughing and hacking against the choking smoke, I helped Jack to his feet. Together we threw our shoulders into the door. It refused to budge. We turned to the walls, but they were just as solid.

We lost track of time.

Jack gasped. "Tony! I can't breathe. I—"

"Down on the floor, Jack. Smoke's not as thick there."

He lay down, gasping for breath. "Tony. My throat. It's burning. I can't—"

I refused to lie down, knowing that if I did, I'd never rise. I continued to throw myself into the door, oblivious to breaking any bones. I felt the door give slightly. I redoubled my efforts.

My breath was coming in short, burning gasps. I kept my eyes closed against the stinging smoke. And then I felt the heat seeping through the walls.

With abandon, I threw my weight against the door. It gave a little more. Time and again, with renewed desperation, I hurled myself against it, feeling it budge a fraction with each blow, but it continued to hold.

I paused, leaning my head against the door. The last words I remember muttering were, "I don't believe this." I backed away and threw myself into the door again and again until an all-encompassing darkness engulfed me.

Next thing I remember was being cold and then hands shaking me awake. I opened my eyes and stared into the most beautiful mixture of mud and snow I'd ever seen. I glanced up, my face feeling the heat of the burning barn twenty-five yards away.

Hands shook me again. "Boudreaux! You okay?"

I rolled over and stared into the face of Lester Taggart!

Chapter Thirty-three

Buck Ford's face appeared from the darkness beside Taggart. "Are you all right, Boudreaux? What in the Sam Hill is going on out here? We saw the fire and came down to see what was taking place."

"Jack! Where's Jack?" Frantically, I scooted around in the snow and found Jack behind me. I scrabbled over to him on my hands and knees just as he broke into spasms of coughing.

I dropped my head to his chest and muttered a short prayer of thanks. Then I remembered Taggart. I pushed to my feet and jabbed a finger at him. "What are you doing here?" I shouted, taking a threatening step in his direction.

Ford stepped in front of me. "Hold on, Boudreaux. This is my cousin I told you about. He's the one who gave me the information I passed on to you." He paused and gave the burning barn a wry look. "Information it appears you ignored."

"Cousin? But—"

Taggart held up his hands. "Cool off, Boudreaux. Danny O'Banion sent me."

"O'Banion?"

"After you had him check on the funeral home business, he called me and hired me to keep an eye on you up here."

Then I remembered Danny's last words. "You sound funny. I'll send someone up there."

I had laughed at that redheaded Irishman and told him no, but he had sent someone anyway. I could hug him.

Danny had made another remark I remembered. About Taggart. Once he took a job, he stuck it out. He was loyal, and that was why he was in demand.

I looked up at Taggart. Right now that bulldog face of his looked like an angel's. "Knowing Danny, that figures." I offered him my hand. "Thanks."

He took it and with a wink replied, "Just doing a job."

"I owe you two guys. Thanks for getting us out."

Ford shook his head. "We didn't. When we got here, you were laying right there."

"Huh?" I looked around at Jack. "Did you drag me out here?"

Sitting in the mud, Jack shook his head, clearly puzzled. "Last I remember is laying down on the floor." He paused. His frown grew deeper. "Wasn't it you?"

"No." I scratched my head. "If I did, I don't remember it."

Ford grinned. "That happens. My pa was bucked off a horse one time. Landed on his head. Got back up on it and broke it. A week later in church, he suddenly asked ma where the horse was. He wanted to get back on and break it. That week was always a blank to the old man until the day he passed on." He continued. "I got me a suspicion, but I'd like to know what happened out here."

I looked from one to the other, then quickly told them the story. When I finished, Ford pursed his lips and nodded. "I figured something. I hated Jim Bob, and I was tickled to see him gone, but I always puzzled over the fact that he did go. His roots was here. It didn't make sense that he just up and took off without saying a word to nobody."

"We've got pictures of Houston's remains in the grave. Of course, knowing the sheriff and Lewis, they might have already dug the coffin up and disposed of them."

Taggart shook his head and grinned. "Nope. It's still there."

I looked at him. "How do you know?"

"I've been watching."

A tiny grin played over my face. "Thanks again."

Headlights turned off the highway onto Cemetery Road.

"Looks like we're fixing to have a visitor," Ford muttered. "So now what?"

Moments later two more sets of headlights turned onto the road. "A crowd is more likely," Taggart said.

"All right. One of them is bound to be the sheriff. "You and Taggart just stand where you are. You saw the fire, and you came to see what was going on. Jack and I are going to hide in the bushes over here. Maybe the sheriff will be so surprised to see us that he'll give himself away."

Taggart arched an eyebrow. "What if he don't?"

"I still have the pictures of the grave."

"He'll find some way to sneak out of that."

Then I had an idea. "Maybe not, Buck. Maybe not. Us city boys got some smarts too."

Lights swept across the countryside as a car pulled into the drive. To my surprise, it was Gabe and Mabel Hooker. Moments later, Sheriff Perry pulled in, followed by Newt Gibons. Almost the whole town had turned out.

Mabel and Gabe sloshed through the snow to Ford and Taggart, followed moments later by Sheriff Perry, who came to stand beside them. "What's going on here?"

"Don't know, Gus. My cousin here and me saw the fire and pulled in.

"Same here, Gus," Mabel put in.

Perry shook his head. "Bums. Transients probably tried to spend the night and started a fire. You folks can go on home. I'll take care of it."

Gabe and Mabel started to turn around, but Ford said, "That's all right, Gus. We'd like to watch for a while if you don't mind." He chuckled. "After all, the only thing around here we ever see exciting is TV."

Momentarily flustered, Perry shrugged. "Have it your way. Don't blame me if you get burned or something."

The fire slowly burned down. Once, Gabe turned to leave, but Ford shook his head behind the sheriff's back. Gabe frowned, then whispered to his wife. They both remained.

Soon the barn was nothing but smoking embers lit by the beams of a few flashlights.

Perry shrugged and turned to the others. "Looks like that's it, folks. We might as well head back home."

"What about the transients, Sheriff? You want me to help you look through the ashes? We got flashlights, and we can all turn on our headlights."

Perry stammered. "Oh, I—I can do that tomorrow, when it's light."

Gabe Hooker spoke up. "I kinda hate to leave anybody out here on a night like this, Sheriff, even if he is dead. You know what I mean? It don't seem Christian."

The sheriff gave in. "Well, let me do it. I don't want none of you burned."

I heard Buck Ford whisper to Gabe and Mabel, "Watch him go straight to where the seed room was."

Sheriff Perry went directly to the seed room. After a few moments, he searched the rest of the ashes. Ten minutes later, he returned, clearly puzzled. "Looks like I was wrong. I didn't see no one in there."

Jack and I rose from the underbrush. "Does that surprise you, Sheriff Perry?"

His flashlight beam hit us. "You! But—"

Holding a hand before my eyes to block the light, I sloshed through the snow. "But what? You figured we'd be where you left us, in the seed room?"

Sharp gasps came from the Hookers and Newt Gibons.

The sheriff puffed up. Belligerently, he responded, "I don't know what you're talking about, Boudreaux."

"Come on, Sheriff. It's over. Buck Ford knows about it. His cousin knows. I know. Jack knows. In two minutes, the Hookers and Newt Gibons will know. What are you going to do, kill us all like you and Marvin Lewis killed Jim Bob Houston twenty years ago and Justin Chester a couple weeks back? It's over."

Keeping my eyes on him, I retold the story for Newt and the Hookers. I added, "Justin had no idea Houston's body was in the spaceman's grave. All he wanted to do was dig it up to see if the spaceman was there or not, but the sheriff and Lewis had to stop him. Jack and I figured it out, and that's why the sheriff and Lewis locked us in the seed room and tried to murder us."

Perry's eyes blazed. His nostrils flared. "That's a lie."

"Is it?"

"Yeah."

"Then suppose you empty your pockets."

Taken aback by my request, he frowned. "Huh? What for?"

"What's the matter, Sheriff? Afraid?"

I kept my fingers crossed, hoping the sheriff was as dumb as I thought.

He snorted. "All right." He jammed his hand into his left pocket and pulled out a rumpled handkerchief. "Satisfied?"

"The other one."

He switched his flashlight to his left and angrily jammed his hand into his pocket and froze.

I leaped forward, grabbing his wrist, holding his hand in his pocket. He slammed the flashlight onto my back twice before Buck grabbed his arm. Together we threw the struggling sheriff to the ground.

"Put the light on his right hand," I said, pulling his hand out. I had to force his fingers open. There lay the Case knife my grandfather had given me. "Recognize that, Buck?"

He picked up the knife and studied it, spotting the missing shield on the handle. "That's your knife, the one from your grandpa."

"Yeah. The one Perry took from my pocket before setting the barn on fire."

Suddenly, Sheriff Perry went limp.

I rose.

Ford leaned over and pulled Perry's service revolver from his holster. "I don't know if this is legal or not," he said, rising to his feet, "but now that we don't have a sheriff, I figure a citizen can take his place until things are straightened out. My cousin and me are going to lock the sheriff in his jail, then go up and get Marv Lewis. Gabe, you and Mabel drive over to the sheriff in Reuben and tell him what's going on. I suppose he'll have to tell us what to do next."

We spent the remainder of the night at the sheriff's office, telling our story half a dozen times and then repeating it once again to the Texas Ranger assigned to the area.

I had forgotten all about the UFO nonsense until I overheard Gabe Hooker tell one of the officers that the fire was so hot that it even melted some of the seed bins on the seed drill. Later, I asked Gabe what he meant by seed bin. He explained. "Some folks call them hoppers, some call them bins. You know, they're shaped like a funnel with a large top. That's what they put the seed in to plant it."

Jack and I looked at each other, both remembering Barton's claim that he had hidden the items on the inventory list in a seed bin. We figured he meant the seed room, but I remembered seeing all of the old rusty farm implements on one side of the barn, and there in the middle was a seed drill with a dozen hoppers across the back.

As the sun rose, we pulled into Barton's drive and around behind his old house. We hurried to the barn, sloshing through snow made crisp by the freezing night. "There it is." I pointed to the seed drill, which was nothing more than a hulk of burned metal among the smoking timbers.

One of the large beams of the barn had fallen directly onto the hoppers, smashing them. I kicked the charred remains off, then searched one shattered bin after the other. In the mud beneath one, I discovered several chunks of metal, and then, beneath the surface of the mud, my fingers touched a small sheet of metal, four inches by five.

I wiped the mud from it. The fire had distorted the small piece. When I bent it, it remained bent.

Jack looked over my shoulder. "Is that it? Huh, is it?"

Without answering I handed it to him. I stared at the pieces of metal in my hand. I started to throw them away, but then I realized, these were items Justin Chester had held precious. I dropped them into my pocket, mud and all. Hey, I could always clean the jacket.

We picked our way out of the barn to where we had lain the night before. Jack exclaimed. "Hey, look! There's those same tracks again."

I looked around to where Jack was pointing under a canopy of elm trees. There, a couple of tadpole-shaped imprints were headed in the direction of the Diablo Canyons. Then I noticed one of the odd imprints heading in a different direction, into the barn.

"What do you think they are, Tony, huh?"

Shaking my head, I grunted. "I told you. Tumbleweeds. Something like that. That's all. Not tracks."

Jack retorted. "Naw. Those are spaceman tracks. The spaceman is the one who pulled us from the fire."

All I could do was shake my head in frustration.

"No. It was either you or me that pulled us out, Jack. That's all it could be."

A couple of days later, George McDaniel, the interim sheriff, told us we could leave. As we packed, Jack grinned.

"Hey, I can't wait to get back to Austin. You going to follow me?"

I thought of all the good people in Elysian Hills I had met. For some strange reason, I hated to leave. "No. You go on. I want tell a few folks good-bye."

Sam Fuqua had tears in his eyes. I did too. Newt was his usual reserved self. Mabel had to give me a hug and an invitation to come back anytime. Ford almost crushed my hand when he shook it. Taggert had already pulled out, but Buck told me that Taggart had overheard Perry telling Lewis he had paid to have my brake line cut.

Fuqua had asked, "What do you think will happen to them, Boudreaux? You're around this kind of thing all the time."

I laughed. "Anyone's guess. Jim Bob's so far in the past, only a confession will nail them on that. Chester might be a little different. Lewis has to explain how the setting of his ring got into the wrecked truck. And, who knows? He might explain that away." I offered him my hand. "I wish I could say that justice will be done, but I can't. You take care, you hear?"

He grinned. "You too. You ever back up around here, I'll be sorely disappointed if you don't stop by for dinner."

Instead of heading straight back to the interstate, I took Cemetery Road, knowing it would intersect the interstate a few miles south. I slowed as I passed the winding creek and stopped in front Barton's old house for one last look. A gust of wind rattled the broken shutters against the weathered clapboard. I felt as if I were leaving a good friend behind.

My last glimpse of Elysian Hills was the cemetery.

* * *

I drove into Austin in midafternoon. My first stop was Tricia Chester, where I dropped off Justin's belongings—all except the items on the inventory list. She shed tears when I told her that Justin had been murdered. I gave her the details, cautioning her that she would be getting calls from various agencies in North Texas.

And, as I expected, a self-righteously chagrined Frank Chester called that evening, demanding information. I told him what I had told his sister. I hung up the receiver, wondering if he truly believed he was fooling anyone.

What a family. Justin deserved better.

Jack called me the next morning. He had cleaned the sheet of metal, and on the bottom were the same characters Justin had written on his notes. But the metal didn't respond as Justin had claimed. Had the fire destroyed one of its qualities, or had Justin simply been mistaken? If he were mistaken, what about Sam Fuqua? What about Harlan Barton? They had both seen the metal crumpled and returned to it original shape.

"Do you want it, Tony?"

"What? The sheet of metal?"

"Yeah."

"No. You keep it. A memento of the alien spaceman."

He snorted. "Well, you can laugh if you want, but stop and think. You didn't haul us out. I didn't, so who did? And what about those tracks? Remember when we saw some a couple of days before just like them, heading back to the canyon?"

"Come on, Jack. There's no such thing as aliens. I must have done it and just don't remember."

"Well, you think what you want. I'll always believe it was

that little spaceman who pulled us out of the fire." He paused, then added in a low voice, "You know, Tony, I can't help wondering what the little space guy will do now that Harlan Barton is gone."

I shook my head. I was tired of arguing with him. "See you around, Jack. Tell Diane I said hi."

After we hung up, I looked at the other scraps of metal on my kitchen snack bar. I knew as sure as I was sitting there, if I gave them to the Chesters, within weeks they would be discarded, just as they had discarded Justin.

Instead, I washed them off, dropped them into a glass, and set it on my bookcase. "There you are, Justin. You can rest easy. Someone will always remember you and your little alien."

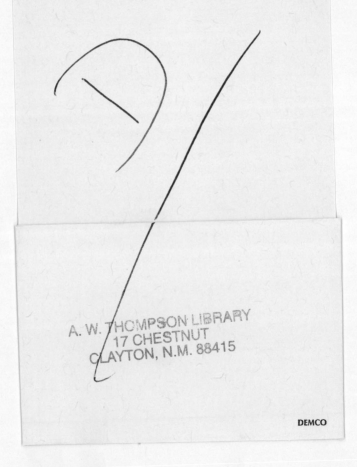